i cope.

CCM Design & Cover by *Michael J Seidlinger*

ISBN – 978-0-9846037-7-0

Find yourself

Through innovative fiction

A coping mechanism perfect for your needs.

http://copingmechanisms.net

:::Best Behavior:::

—Noah Cicero—

Introduction

For a week straight in January of 2009 I went with a book bag full of classic American literature to the Waffle House. I drank coffee and ate the same thing every night. I ate one waffle, two sausage patties, two over-easy eggs, and grits. I ate my grits with butter and sugar.

The books I brought with me were *The Sun Also Rises* by Ernest Hemingway, *The Great Gatsby* by F. Scott Fitzgerald, *On the Road* by Jack Kerouac, *Naked Lunch* by William S. Burroughs, *The Naked and the Dead* by Norman Mailer, *Revolutionary Road* by Richard Yates, *The Bell Jar* by Sylvia Plath, *One Flew over the Cuckoo's Nest* by Ken Kesey, *Fear and Loathing in Las Vegas* by Hunter S. Thompson, *Trout Fishing in America* by Richard Brautigan, *In Cold Blood* by Truman Capote, *Rules of Attraction* by Bret Easton Ellis, and *Bright Lights, Big City* by Jay McInerney.

I would show up at the Waffle House off I-80 in Hubbard at 12:30AM, place the books on the table.

The server would ask, "Noah, what are you doing?"

I would respond, "I'm doing important research."

I wanted to write a book. A book that would define a generation. Why I would want to do that, I don't know. Probably boredom. Sometimes people get bored and think that it would be good to keep busy by writing a novel that defines a generation.

She would say, "My son wouldn't stop vomiting today." I'd respond, "Did you take him to the doctor?" The server would respond, "Yeah, got a script for antibiotics. he'll probably be better tomorrow." Then the server would go away.

Every night I would read through the books, trying to decipher, attempting to get the secret knowledge that enabled the aforementioned authors to write a novel that defined a generation. Usually I would be in very deep thought and the server would say, "Noah, do you need some more coffee?" I would look up and say, "Yes, please." The server would pour me more coffee. I would drink the coffee. Hours would pass. Sometimes I would knock my head on the books. Truckers eating scrambled eggs and waffles would laugh. Twice I started crying. Ernest Hemingway kept making fun of me. F. Scott Fitzgerald got drunk and threw up in my car. William Faulkner, John Steinbeck, Saul Bellow, and Phillip Roth sent me emails asking why they weren't in my book bag.

I tried to remember the first time I read each book. I was still in high school when I read *The Sun Also Rises* and *On the Road*. They made me very excited about life. The books assumed that life was really great and that happiness was awesome. I learned recently that much of the 20th Century's happiness was caused by the industrial use of oil, natural gas and coal. Which led to a food surplus. Which meant these old great novels where the reader is supposed to assume that the zeitgeist is creating all this new happiness, it is actually false and that many of the books of the 20th Century can be shelved under, "Massive Oil use and its Effects on Humans."

When I was sitting at the Waffle House those nights in January of 2009 I had a pretty cynical view of reality. I had just read *Guns, Germs and Steel* by Jared Diamond, *The Medieval World* by Norman Cantor, *The Long Emergency* by James Howard Kunstler and *Pimp* by Iceberg Slim. Those books helped me view the world as a pile of shit where there was no spiritual value to anything, everybody just did things that made them feel better, everyone, like all the people of earth and even animals have their own private absurd version of reality. Also that human life depends upon resources, good soil, and governments with just procedures.

Writing a novel that defined a generation would not be easy. I knew that. I knew I needed things. I needed to have a generation. According to the Internet since the characters in this novel are all born between 1980 and 1985 this novel is about Generation Y. Some people call this generation the Millennial Generation. I personally would like to name my generation, it has always been a dream of mine: here are some ideas:

People who like Gadgets Generation
(Can be shortened to Gadget Generation)
Text Message Generation
Graduate College with no Jobs Generation
Internet Porn Generation
iPod Generation

Cigarettes got really Expensive so everyone Stopped Smoking Generation

Some went to War, Some went to College, some just Hung Out Generation

Ironic Generation

These slogans will never be picked up. They aren't flashy and short. But Ironic Generation might work.

None of the books helped. They did not help because they were books not about my generation. I personally do not exactly know what the word 'generation' means. I assume the word 'generation' implies a collection of people that were born and raised during certain eras in specific countries by a previous generation that has their own special name. But there are constants between the generations that must be recognized, everybody from every generation shits, eats, needs shelter, has sex, and doesn't enjoy when bad things happen.

So the questions are: how do they shit, how did they inhabit those shelters, how did they have sex, and respond to bad things. I guess those are the questions, and here is a really long answer:

Best Behavior

This book was written to Of Montreal's "The Past is a Grotesque Animal".

illustration by Sam Pink

Best Behavior

1.

"Then she threw everything off the shelf at my head," said Tony.

We were sitting at Denny's at three in the morning after drinking at several bars. Tony's face seemed completely calm. The man had a master's degree with honors and over 50 thousand dollars worth of college loan debt.

Tony's face looked older. I've known him for years. Twice a year he comes back home from New Mexico and looks older. I wondered if I looked older. I'm 28, he's like 26. Time has passed. We've accomplished things. He has a masters, I have four books published. He's had like 200 hundred girlfriends, all with the beginning, middle and end. I almost got married to a woman but that experiment failed. Now I live with another woman named Amanda, much different from the last, in appearance and psychological makeup. But we aren't lovers. I realized on a Thursday in 05 while washing my hair that I needed a friend more than a lover. So we became friends and not lovers

"Then I grabbed her neck," said Tony.

Tony kept saying strange things to me about domestic violence and a rich girl that went to New York City to become a lawyer.

Then Tony said, "She was like a child."

That sounded strange to me. *Like a child.* I've met these women all my life. I've met those men all my life. Children. Adults behaving like children. But the child he was referencing got excellent grades and was going to become a lawyer. She was what the world called *A good kid.* The Teacher's pet. The kid who got all the stars. The kid who grew up in the gated community with a doctor or business owner for a dad. This girl throws books at Tony's head.

"She grew a garden but let everything die."

I thought what kind of person lets a garden die?

I said, "But you seem so nice when you're around me."

He said, "Maybe there's a secret me you don't know about."

"There probably is."

"One time we fought for hours."

"What started the fight?"

He looks up trying to remember the initiation and said, "I don't remember. I can't honestly name what started the fights. I remember the fights, but not what started them."

"Nothing serious."

"No, nothing serious like bills or anything that concerned life. Usually she ruminated about being fat till I couldn't take it anymore. Or she would be really mad about the dog."

"How does one start a violent fight about a dog," I said in amazement.

"With great skill and determination." He continued, "We were fighting on the couch, she kept hitting me," he makes punching motions with his hands. "So I held her hands down and she said, 'do you want to marry me?' I responded, 'maybe someday.' "Then she got really mad and started kicking me, but it was funny because I was holding her arms and we were on a couch. I didn't laugh out loud or anything, but I was laughing in my head. So I wrestled her down to the floor and sat on her chest and called her a stupid bitch. That didn't help the situation at all. So I got off her and went to the kitchen and got a small but sharp knife from the kitchen."

"You were going to kill her?"

"That occurred to me, but I felt guilt from my father and The Holy Roman Catholic Church and discarded that idea. Instead of killing her I angrily sat on the couch and stabbed the knife into my calf." He pulled up his pant leg to show me the scar.

"That sounds dramatic."

"It was. It stopped the fight though."

Most people have *secret mes*. Jealousy got hold of him. He was a control freak. People who get master's degrees with honors are usually control freaks. People who control their lives are control freaks. You have to be. Capitalism demands responsibility, and responsibility demands that the human who wants a stable well-ordered life takes control over their emotions and behaviors to achieve their goals in life. He ended with school loans and a job working for the state in a library. I don't know if that constitutes as the making of one's destiny. He has a place to live, food on the table, a car, the bills are paid on time, and he can meet women easily. I admire the man. He came from good Rust Belt stock, divorced parents, a marine father who works at the Post Office and a mother who worked through college and became an engineer, but just got laid off because the Chevy wasn't selling cars anymore..

Things had changed since I saw Tony in the summer. Gas prices were over four dollars then. Now they are below two. The economy had collapsed. A lot of people were getting laid off and if you weren't personally, you knew somebody that was. A lot of people had foreclosed on their house, and if you didn't, you knew somebody that did. There was fear everywhere. We had voted in Barack Obama, the Bush years were soon to be over. Something strange started happening.

Tony got a text message from his male roommate, "Text Ashley, she's wondering what you're doing."

Tony went to the bathroom and texted her.

While he was gone I looked around.

There was a man in his thirties so drunk at the counter he could barely move. An overweight woman sat next to him propping him up. He looked like he wanted to go to sleep.

Everyone else in the section was black and talking on their cell phones instead of to each other.

Tony returned and said, "I called her. But I bet she's fucking my other roommate right now. They only did that to convince me they aren't fucking."

"One should always assume a conspiracy."

"I'm sure of it."

"Guilty before proven innocent."

Tony smiled.

We laughed.

Told Tony about going back to college. I went when I was younger. I stopped going after four semesters because I didn't want to make my parents happy. I didn't believe them that college mattered. I didn't believe them because none of the things they told me made sense, so why should that. But time passed. Worked one sad job after another. Not hard jobs. Usually cook or pizza boy. The cooking made me sweat in the summer but it doesn't hurt to sweat every once and awhile. But there was never any money. I was 28. And I had never made more than 10 dollars an hour. I hadn't had a real bank account in years. I made 2,000 writing the year before. There didn't seem a reason for me to make money. I had never gotten married or had children. There was no one to support. No one looked up to me. No one needed me. So I decided on a Thursday while washing my hair that I should need myself. It was a struggle to return to a place of motivation. I had defaulted on my loans and had to pay them perfectly for nine months in a row. After that was accomplished I was allowed to return to the academic arena with help from the Pell Grant. I was so poor the government was paying almost all of it. I was going back with 10,000 dollars in student loans. That was the song of life, loans, money, and trying to get things done.

2.

Tony drove me home in his mom's beautiful new Chevy. The interior lights were amazing. It was the only thing amazing about the car. The rest of it was normal. There were seats, a steering wheel, and a cup holder. Tony's mom got a DUI in that car last year.

Tony said, "I almost joined the Marines earlier this year."

I laughed.

"I went to the recruiter like five times."

"But why the Marines, you seem like an air-force guy."

"Why do you think?"

"Oh... Your father."

He didn't respond immediately and said, "The Marines are easier to get to fly jets with."

"I didn't know you wanted to fight terrorists."

"I didn't want to fight terrorists. It's okay now. My dad and I got drunk last night with my mom. He said to me, 'You're a good boy.' I'm okay now."

"Our fathers. They are like a shadow that hangs over us boys."

"I have his nose."

"Romulus and Remus, Buddha, and Jesus didn't have fathers. There was no shadow cast on them. They looked into the mirror and saw no nose of a father."

"My father tried to touch my mother and she started yelling at him, 'if you keep touching me, you'll have to leave.'"

"That's funny."

He didn't respond, so I said, "My father always wanted to be free of narcissistic women, he wanted to be a cowboy, he wanted to be free. To live the way he wanted. I always felt that his life was showing me that he wanted to live a different life. He didn't want to be a simple Sicilian from Warren, but a man with his own rules and logic. But he never escaped. Never could throw it down and have faith in his secret choices. I became that dream, but he could not accept that."

"My father didn't want to have a kid while in high school, and I'm 25 without child. He wanted to be educated and I have become those things. He accepted it, but while being very drunk he told me that him and my mother decided to help me get through school because I had to learn what it meant to be an adult, it means bills, and struggle."

"Our fathers will never leave us."

"No they won't."

We ended up in my driveway eventually.

We gave each other strong manly hugs. He said, "See ya, merry Christmas."

I left the car remembering when he left to New Mexico. It was a sunny day in the August. He came over for a little bit. We sat on my porch and had a final conversation. I cried a little bit seeing him go. Then he drove away like he did that night. It was December, it was cold, we were wearing winter coats and rubbing our hands together.

He was gone again.

All my friends had gone.

My best friend from high school Sidney was gone to Columbus. My first love married with a kid in Warren and she never speaks to me. Saw her once and she ran from me. My favorite family member, my brother, gone, dead. Walked in the house. Took off my coat and hung it on a hanger. Sat at the kitchen table and took my boats off and placed them neatly where the shoes go. The heat kicked on. The house would be warm and comfortable soon. My roommate Amanda wasn't home. She was gone, somewhere in Cleveland listening to her Jewish friend sing Christmas songs with a man named Joseph. I walked to the computer and checked my email.

3.

I met Amanda five years ago in a bar. Was 22 and had just returned from Eugene, Oregon. I had previously finished a seven year on and off again relationship with a very narcissistic woman. Amanda had previously finished a three relationship with a guy who was suffering from schizophrenia. We were both ready to move on to functional people. Most people considered us weird, but we were functional.

I saw her sitting in a bar holding a drink looking nervous and sad. A band was playing. What band I don't recall. She was tall with bleach blond hair hanging down to her shoulders. She was wearing a green shirt and black skirt. She looked beautiful. I thought, 'I want to talk to her tonight.'

At that time in my life I was hitting on girls constantly and was mildly successful. I ended up in several apartments having decent sex. But none of the people seemed at the same place I was. It was just people having sex with each other, that was all. No desire for a relationship or procreation. We were lonely and felt forgotten. Most of us had not gone to college or were dropouts. We weren't people full of dreams, we were underpaid, and had no outlet for attention. So we would get drunk and pay attention to each other.

Amanda and I flirted and it didn't seem like anything. We did get along. But people get along all the time.

Three weeks later I moved in her house. Amanda lived in a house owned by parents and didn't have to pay rent. She lived with a Jewish girl named Dedra in her senior year of college. I only mention that she was Jewish because she was very into studying Judaism, the holocaust, and even the Jewish massacres of Medieval times. She left the house eventually to get her masters in Judaic Studies and then to work at a synagogue. And after 7 years I was still living there.

Amanda had spent the last seven years of her life trying to graduate college. She graduated ninth in a class of 300 kids. She even scored out of her foreign language requirements. But Amanda like many people of her generation kept picking new majors. She was an English major at the beginning, then she was a linguistics major, then a sociology major, then an English teacher major, then she settled on Hospitality Management. She wanted to own her own restaurant or maybe a small hotel on the side of the highway in Kansas. Or maybe get one of those District Manager jobs where they give you a new car and have you drive around from business to business all day stopping in for a couple of hours, torturing everybody about rules, regulations, product cost, labor cost, invoices, and who gets and doesn't get a raise and how much do they get.

Amanda didn't know what to do with her life. That phrase was said a lot this past decade. People back in the day didn't do things with their lives. They went where the jobs were. They went to the coal mines, to the factories, to the good soil. But the world had changed in the last 50 years. We had choices now. We could choose what type of job we wanted to do. This was unusual to humans. Perhaps as unusual to the tribes of Northern Europe when the Romans showed up and said, "Look, we need organization, laws, and ownership." The Northern Europeans stared them and stumbled through it for 1000 years before getting it right.

Our parents didn't know what to do with us. They didn't have a choice either. Most of them went to the areas with jobs and took the first one they could get, and worked their way up to management. Even if they were white collar, the same thing applied, they went where the jobs were. They took the job and worked to get raises.

Things were different now.

Now, in that strange place called America a person could choose what their role in society would be. But we didn't think about it as a role. We thought about as, "How we want to live." We didn't discuss roles, it was too Catholic, too Medieval. Instead of role we had status and prestige. Instead of a job being what a human did to benefit their society, it became a psychological symbol of status. People wanted to become lawyers because prestige and money went along with it. People wanted to become social workers and school teachers because that would represent they had some money but were getting the money from helping people. People wanted to become businessmen for money to buy impressive things. People wanted to become managers of restaurants, auto-body shops, hotels, and Wal-Marts because that would show they were in a position of power and it supplied enough money to buy houses and feed the children. And of course there was still *the rabble*. The rabble worked the low paying jobs, trying to feed themselves and their children. Even though they were poor and had little opportunity to become white collar there were still many programs to get them to become nurses, truck drivers, construction workers and auto-mechanics. Because the new cars were so complicated the job of auto-mechanic became a job that paid well and even had a little prestige. One would notice that I omitted the job of doctor. My generation gave up on the dream of being a doctor several years back. Going to medical school was too expensive even for white collar children, so America began to import doctors from India and South America where medical school was much cheaper. The ideal of a doctor being a person that helps somehow disappeared from the American landscape. Instead it got turned into a money making device and turned off would be doctors, instead opting out for social worker jobs and nursing. People began to see doctors as agents of insurance and pill companies and not people trying to cure the sick. The role of the doctor was lost in America, and India with its billion people was glad to send us some of theirs to replace our lost doctors.

Amanda sat in the little kitchen with aged portraits of butterflies on the wall, a sink covered in rust stains. A refrigerator with magnets holding up articles we had written together, pictures her nephews had drawn for her, and postcards from friends that had moved away. It was a sad kitchen, not a new modern one. I remember this story by an old black woman I once worked with how her father used to sit in the kitchen at six in the morning, drink coffee and read the bible everyday. I remember when I was young my dad's friends used to come over and they would drink beer, and my dad would pull out a bottle of whiskey from underneath the kitchen sink. They would sit and drink the whiskey and feel good, they would talk about previous times. About stores that didn't exist anymore, about people that moved or drifted away. It was a kitchen like that. The kind an old black man could read the bible in or the kind friends could drink whiskey and talk about the past.

Amanda sat in that kitchen. She wrote out bills. Staring at the numbers, thinking about money. She didn't feel like doing the bills. She didn't feel like giving anyone her money. But she rationalized that electricity and heat are important things and must be maintained to live a good life.

Amanda began to cry. She wasn't balling or wailing. They were just tears. They came out of the corner of her eyes and slid over her white cheeks. A crying woman. My life has been spent next to crying women. My mother cried, my grandmother cried, my female co-workers cry. I learned young that it was not easy being a woman or black in America. Being treated second class was not good for one's emotional state. Life was harder for them. It was easy to see that.

I heard her crying from the living room while I checked Hipster Runoff. I've heard her cry a million times, about how she doesn't want to be like her mother, and her father having diabetes. But these tears were different. Each one of her cries had their own distinct tears and sounds that went along with it. It was a cry of fear and anguish.

I sat there for awhile and listened. Amanda was not the type of person that needed someone to interrogate her when she cried. But I believed she was crying over false notions concerning her reality so I stood and walked slowly to the kitchen.

When I entered she was looking down writing checks. I sat down across from her and didn't say anything. She kept crying like I wasn't there. Like it was none of my business.

I said, "Amanda?"

"Yes," she said like she wasn't crying.

"Are you all right?"

"I'm okay."

"You don't look okay."

"I graduated college."

"I know, I'm proud of you."

"Yeah, but like."

"Like what?"

"I've been going to school since I was five."

"Well, it's over now. Make money, buy Ikea and a flat screen television."

She paused and said, "I'm okay."

She wasn't going to say it. She was worried. Her life had taken on a new meaning. She had a received new status that could never be taken away. *A person with a bachelor's degree.* She was white collar. If she wanted she could make more money than her parents. She would make more money than the people she grew up with. People would look at her differently. She wasn't a loser, she was educated. But she had lived for 26 years as a poor blue collar girl surrounded by poor blue collar people. She had transcended them. And by transcending them she had said that somehow their life was not as good as hers. She didn't hate their life. They wanted her to be successful. They wanted her to become a person that was financially capable of taking care of herself. And this was the era of jobs that required training.

There were other worries though: she barely knew anyone that had graduated college. She had very little idea of how one lived being white collar making good money. She didn't know what her life could become. But it was deeper that, she had always been a child, never fully responsible. But now she was condemned to be responsible, she was an adult and educated. She was a person that knew how to do something, that knew things about the world, people she had never met before would be impressed when she announced that she was educated, would instantly assume that she was a responsible hard working individual. There is something scary about being assumed responsible. At least when one is assumed irresponsible there is nothing to live up to, but assumed responsibility creates a tension in oneself that you must behave to certain standards.

Amanda was crying. I could do nothing to make her stop and there was no apparent reason for her to stop. She had nothing planned, she had all evening to cry. Amanda had a new life. A new status to become and new money to be made. It was something she had to deal with alone. I left the kitchen and went back to checking Blogs.

4.

I was going to New York City early the next morning to be interviewed with several other writers for a hipster magazine aimed toward females. I had never heard of the magazine. Everyone kept telling me it was very popular and the article would sell books. I didn't care what the magazine was. If they sold five couples or five million. There was a need to escape Youngstown. There was a need to get on a Greyhound and travel somewhere. Things had gotten bad. Amanda's dad was laid off. The car was broke. My job wasn't giving out raises. The news said everyday that life was getting worse. It was a hard year. Gas hit over four dollars a gallon. Huge banks considered Gods on the American landscape had collapsed. Trillions in wealth had been lost. I lost my little quarter raises. A lot of people lost their 401ks and a lot lost their jobs. Amanda had good credit but she couldn't even get a loan for 3,000 dollars. In 07 they were sending her letters in the mail to get business loans. Those letters no longer came. Things had changed very quickly.

I had been to New York City several times before: one time before I was even a writer. I went there as a person with barely any money. I was escaping then too. A woman I hadn't seen in years, her name was May. There was this moment May and I had in a bar on New Year's 2001. We were drinking with friends. We kept saying with sincerity that we couldn't imagine being without each other. That our fate was linked. That we would die knowing and holding each other. That we loved each other and life would not make that different. We disappeared from each other's lives. I would look around the room and she was not there. I would come home from work and she was not there. When the phone rang, it was never her. She was gone. She had gotten married and had a child. I was still not married and without child. I was still adrift. Still stumbling. Her sister said May wasn't happy. May wouldn't sleep in the same room as her husband. They stayed married for the kid. Or because they felt like that was what life was supposed to be. The woman I loved so much was gone. We convince ourselves of crazy things sometimes. When I would walk through the mall I would always look for her, hoping to see her pass by. I didn't want to talk to her. Didn't want to touch her. There was a desire to be with her. I wanted to see her alive, her *being*, to see that thing, that made me fall in love with her. It is not easy to fall in love. It is nice to be reminded of what it takes for that to happen. But perhaps what she did that enabled me to fall in love with her, would no longer be there, or what was in me, that enabled it, would no longer be there.

I left May and went to New York City. I didn't have friends in New York City then so I slept in my car on the side of the street. I parked my car on the Bowery. The Bowery was always mentioned in novels so I thought it was the place to go. I walked around and looked at the tall buildings, walked around Times Square and walked all the way down to Ground Zero. Ground Zero didn't look like much then. It was mostly cleaned up. People always tell their 9-11 story. I've never told mine. Because I don't have one. I was going to college, woke up to the sound of an alarm. Went to the living room and my mother was watching it on television. It didn't seem real. I didn't cry. America was attacked. Life had always seemed capable of getting worse.

The last few trips to New York City were for readings. I read at the KGB to crowded rooms. They weren't all there to see me. They had nothing else to do. For one reading it was snowing outside. It was pretty. The reading was taped and put on Youtube and had over 6,000 views. I was starting to become slightly famous. I didn't feel famous. My books had been translated into German and Polish. But it didn't make a difference in my life. Some money had come in that year. Around 2,000 dollars. It was money badly needed and spent quickly on car parts. I had four books published, been reviewed in Bookslut by a writer that appeared on The Today Show, had a good blurb by a famous comic book artist that had a movie about him, even was mentioned in The Guardian. But there was no difference. I was still cooking at a restaurant. I wasn't even a shift manager. I was getting paid a little more than minimum wage, I was so poor I got the Pell Grant to go to school and when I went to the hospital they gave me care for free. I was a starving artist even though I didn't want to be. My diet consisted of double cheeseburgers from McDonalds and what I could steal from the steak house where I worked. Strangely, I was never overtaken by misery. The people I worked with were on drugs and drank a lot. They didn't have any real hobbies or love for life. I had hobbies that boosted my self-esteem and gave me something to be proud of, from writing to playing the ukulele. I had a small fan base that would write me emails telling me I was a worthwhile human. There were reasons for me to keep existing. Also had shelter, an air-conditioning unit, heating, and indoor plumbing. Things weren't so bad.

I was going to New York City again. The last time I went there it was to do a reading. The reading went well. Hu Chi, Humphrey O'Mally, Desmond Tondo, Lucy McCartney and John Walters were there. All semi-famous writers, with literary dreams. Not dreams to make it big like John Grishman. But dreams to earn money, have a fan base, and announce themselves as writers and not as dog walkers, office workers or MFA teachers. There was a girl there I was going to meet that had emailed me from Myspace.com. Her name was Lin. She liked my books. She was my first female fan that wanted to meet me. I felt like Norman Mailer. I didn't expect her to show up to the reading at all. She was pleasant, intellectual, ambitious. She had a job working for television. Lin was from Minnesota. She had attended an arts school and decided to try to be a New Yorker. We went to a Korean movie about a man with a gun for a penis. Then we went drinking. We had a good time. She had read Knut Hamsun's *Growth of the Soil.* I found it very attractive that she had read Knut Hamsun. We rode on the subway drunk back to her place in Queens. Lin had a personality that went well with mine. She understood sarcasm and that humans were absurd. We could sit on the subway, one of us gesture to a person, and the other would know perfectly what the other one was thinking, that the other person was funny, weird, or sad.

Barely anyone was on the subway and the lighting was horrible. We walked back to her apartment in the night. I thought she would sleep with me. I expected it. But she didn't. I slept on a small couch. It was not that I was mad at her for not sleeping with me. I was mad because she didn't announce that she wouldn't at the beginning of the event. Many months later I wrote a Blog post that she considered about her. It was a mean Blog post. Her friend decided who was part of the elite of hipster New Yorkers decide to find ways to hate me through the Internet. We fought. I wondered if I would see Lin in New York. I knew she was still friends with Hu Chi. So there might be a chance. I didn't hate her. But I knew she hated me. I wondered if I would see her there.

My trips to New York City were always strange to me. I was never a big city person. When money was saved I would take trips to the Colorado Rockies or the Redwoods. I would sleep in tents and drive down highways surrounded by fields of corn. The open landscapes of the west always eased my sense of claustrophobia while New York City always heightened it. New York City is where a person goes to buy things, get a dream job, become an artist, work with stocks, and party. It wasn't a place where a person went to ease their mind. To create a reality of harmony for themselves. There was no peace there. But I had been living a peaceful life all year and needed chaos and some frantic days.

5.

     I worked as a dishwasher for a year. I was poor. Making $6.50 an hour until minimum wage went up and I made 7. When the world looked at me, they looked down. After nine months of dish washing they moved me to the cook line. I didn't want to be a cook. They made little bit more money than I did and it was a lot hotter over there. It didn't seem worth it. But I went anyway, at least I would get the prestige of calling myself a cook.

     I cooked and took shit. No one gave me shit as a dishwasher. No one ever went near me. The managers would say hello and that would be it. But as a cook they spoke to you. They yelled at you. You mattered to the establishment. You were vital to how things ran. If they ran smoothly or badly. If you messed up someone would say something.

     All the cooks had been incarcerated but me. They were getting incarcerated all the time. All of them had DUIs and listened to rap music. They smoked weed when they took out the garbage with the permission of the managers. They bet on football and basketball pools. They had romantic relationships full of jealousy and arguments. They had kids and child support. I didn't have any of these things. I was an outsider and couldn't relate. I did my best to be friendly and they did their best to be friendly to me. But their lives had taken a different direction than mine. All of them had grown up poor and not one of them had a stable father figure growing up.

     The servers were a mixture of social classes, they were mostly women. A lot were women in their thirties trying to make some money to stay alive and feed their kids. And the other ones were girls in nursing school or college passing the time using their money to pay their cell phone bills. Most of the people there were drunks. There was a lot of after work drinking and the attaining of DUIs. Nobody really had any hobbies besides exercising and text messaging. They were good people though, courteous and caring in the simple way mankind has always been.

I walked in the back door of work to the prep line. The prep workers were there. A large man who just lost his job at the Craftmade factory. Craftmade started laying off workers several months ago. One of the broil cook's baby momma was laid off from there also. They were making good money with benefits, now she's out of work and he works as a prep cook for minimum wage with no benefits.

I walked by a young woman in her early twenties named Mary who had beautiful blue eyes and only weighed 100 pounds. Her arms were small but strong. She had already been married and divorced, and moved onto a man that beat her, wouldn't work, and didn't take out the garbage. So she moved onto another man, the new one didn't beat her but he would show up during her shift demanding that she gave him a twenty to buy smokes and beer so he could sit around all day playing video games not taking out the garbage either.

Mary looked sad so I said, "You look sad again, what he do now?"

She kept cutting the cores out of the tomatoes and said, "He's cheating on me, of course."

"Did you yell at him?"

"Of course I yelled, I've been yelling at this cell phone all morning."

"Did you forgive him?"

"Yeah, he was drunk."

I laughed a little and walked away. Some people say that getting drunk and cheating on other people isn't a good excuse. But it is when you know that when you've gotten drunk you've had sex with other people and didn't get caught.

Before I got my coat off there she stood, assistant manager Renee, an overweight woman who talks constantly about Weight Watchers, how her father beat her every time she swore or broke things when she was little, how she got married to a man, had a child, the man left to live in a homeless shelter to not pay child support. That how that man still owed her 24 thousand in child support. She barely did anything all day but complain and watch the televisions at the bar but she pretended that she worked harder than everybody there. She loved to say things like, "You would know where it was if it was up your ass," "Stop trying to get that steak to fuck you, and put it on the plate," "What took your smoke break so long, how long does it take to give a blow job?"

I was putting my coat on a hanger and she said, "Oh, look who it is. Finally decided to show up."

I responded sadly, "I'm here ten minutes early."

"Oh my god, whatever."

She walked away. She and I never engaged in a real discussion. She was so obsessed with defending her little reality that she made a joke out of everything and made it impossible to get any sense of enjoyment out of talking with her.

A few months before I had a panic attack. I had just started school and the making of new habits threw me into a mental frenzy. For five years I had gone to work and done nothing else but read. The jobs I had didn't require any real responsibility, thought, or waking up early. My life had changed. Work was not going well. It was busy and everyone was being ignorant to each other. All the servers were screaming for soups, their fried onions, and cheese fries. I felt isolated and alone. Minor chords on a piano were pounded. I was worried that John McCain would win the presidency. The DOW kept dropping, people were getting laid off that I knew and cherished. I was very stressed out. I was cleaning the fryers and a young cook came over and as a joke poked me in the chest and said, "Boy, you better do those fryers right." It was obviously a joke to everyone else, he said it with a smirk on his face. I was so caught up in my own thoughts, in my own life, trying desperately to adjust to new habits I didn't notice. I clenched my fist and looked at him with hate in my eyes. A look of fear came over him. The young cook was a nice guy. He was my friend. A person I considered with warm feelings. A panic attack started; I couldn't breathe and started crying a little. I went outside to smoke. It was night. I laid on the cement and three nursing majors came over and helped me with water and encouraging words. The only cook that came out to help was Diego Jones. He ran to get me water and had a real look of concern on his face. After that I realized that he must have seen a lot of men struggle. He had grown up poor, been to war and prison. Situations where all men break.

Sundays always meant working with the grill cook Andrew. Andrew was 24 and grew up in Warren. Unlike half the people who went to Warren, he graduated. He went to business school after high school but dropped out. Later he got in a car wreck, got sued and owed over 20 thousand dollars. He was the best cook we had and he never let us forget it. He always talked about how other people couldn't hack it, how they couldn't hang, how basically everyone sucked but him. Besides being a good cook he was a good rapper. He didn't aspire to be famous. Sometimes he would daydream about it. But he didn't tell anyone he was going to be famous and didn't have bitches hanging off of both arms or anything like that. He would make his songs at his friend's house and put them on Myspace. Every time he made a new song he would tell everyone to listen to it, and we all would. He had a soft yet tough voice and he could rap with emotion. The songs were typical of 2008 rap, it had themes about money, girls, and nice things. Which he had none of; but you could tell it made him happy to do it. I liked that very much, there were a lot of people I worked with that didn't do anything to make themselves happy but smoke weed and drink. And he had found an outlet for his emotions, which led to him having the confidence to be a better cook and do less drugs and drinking.

Andrew had it bad, though. His mother was a heroin junky and he had no father. He would sometimes describe, without showing emotion, how his mother would shoot up in front of him. How his mother would have huge abscesses where she plunged the needle into her body. Everyone would stare with pained faces while he would tell us these stories. It wasn't the stories exactly, it was the way he said it, like it seemed normal. Like it was normal for a mother to shoot heroin in front of her son. No one had the heart to tell him that it wasn't normal. Even though we all wanted to, no one gave him a hug.

You got the sense that he wanted to be black. A lot of white people had that from the Youngstown and Warren ghettos. A lot of white people, much more than the media shows, grew up in the world of poor black people. The poor black kids had outlets in the media to represent them, musicians, movie stars, sitcoms and politicians. But poor white people weren't represented in the media except maybe as trailer park hicks. But white kids from the ghetto couldn't look up to them. So Andrew looked up to the rappers. And what the rappers exude were the anger and wants of the poor people of the ghetto. Andrew was poor and he would probably die poor, but he was nice and a good worker.

My job that day was to do expo. Expo really wasn't cooking. Andrew the grill man cooked all the steaks and chicken. The only things I cooked were mushrooms and onions. The first thing I did was stock my area. It was important to have a stocked area. The managers didn't care if anyone stocked. They barely ever went near us unless something went wrong. We stocked our areas because it made things easier for ourselves.

There was a rush for awhile. I had to hurry around putting the plates in the pass-window, throwing baked potatoes on them, sweet potatoes, grilled veggies, and french fries. I was sweating and wanting to leave and go on vacation to New York City. Nothing of what was happening mattered to me. I was a robot repeating motions in response to stimuli.

Saw a ticket.

Read ticket.

Four top.

Four adults.

Eating off adult plates.

Grab four adult plates.

Flick them on window.

Read main dish line to see if any fried shrimp was needed to be called to Diego on Fryers.

There was.

"Diego, three fried shrimp."

Diego yells back, "Three fried shrimp."

I have to keep yelling, "Three fried Shrimp," until he calls it back.

Read line below main dish.

That was the side dish line.

It was indented.

Look to what had to be microwaved.

Grilled veggies and broccoli.

Grab broccoli and grilled veggies.

Both in plastic bags made from petroleum.

(Sometimes while putting the veggies in petroleum based bags I would remember an article I read Online on how that might cause cancer.)

I put the bags in the super microwave that would cook food five times faster than a normal house microwave.

Look again at the ticket.

Two plates need baked potatoes.

They weren't plates for people.

Or food that was going to be eaten by my fellow humans.

They were plates that needed to be filled.

Plates that required side dishes.

I went and got the bake potatoes and slapped them on a plate.

The microwave buzzed.

Veggies were done.

Veggies were stuck on plates in little white dishes.

The ticket was complete.

Then I looked and the broil cook had put up four tickets. I had to do the same thing but with four tickets.

Five minutes later Andrew would say, "The ticket is sold."

I would have to stop what I was doing and run over to the plates.

Read the ticket to see what the potatoes needed, not what the customers wanted, but what the potatoes needed.

The potatoes needed sour cream and butter.

I would grab scoopers in hot water and scoop out butter and sour cream then flick them in the potatoes.

Then grab a large ladle and scoop lemon butter onto the steaks to give them a nice shine.

I looked at the top of the ticket to see what the name was and yelled, "Tammy."

I looked around the kitchen and Tammy was nowhere to be found.

There was no server in sight.

So I had to yell, "Runners."

No one came so I yelled, "If no one runs this food it will die and the window will be backed up and everything will be screwed." When I said, "die" I meant that the temperatures of the steaks would rise from medium rare to medium because the steak cooks itself to a new temperature every three to four minutes.

A server came and took the food and the ticket was able to be stabbed.

Another ticket was sold.

That is how my time was spent at the steak house. The tickets would come and I would put the food on the plates and sell them to the servers. The managers would tell us to have pride in our work. I couldn't. I didn't care about steak. I didn't care about the steak house. They didn't give good raises, when they gave raises. The managers weren't awesome, they were generally lazy. The microwaves wouldn't work, the ovens wouldn't work, the grill had parts of it that didn't work, and sometimes dish tank wouldn't work. The place was ghetto and no one cared. I looked Online out of boredom to see who the owners were and found out that one of them lived in a giant castle in Ireland with a moat around it.

After the midday rush was over the dishwasher came in. His name was Frankie. Frankie was a very wide and strong young black man. Frankie was a collection of horrible things nobody would ever want to happen to them in one person. He grew up on the worst street in Youngstown on Evergreen. Evergreen was horrible in the 80s when he was child. And still to that day a person could drive down that street and see nothing but ramshackle houses and poor black people jobless sitting on their porches drinking forties waiting for their lives to change, but not having a clue how to make it happen. They were so psychologically disenfranchised and restricted to their respected slums that they had no idea how to live in the white man's world. When driving down that street the old Hobbes quote rang in one's ears, "The life of man, solitary, poor, nasty, brutish and short."

Frankie had shot someone in high school. It was an infamous shootout between high school kids in the late 90s. Youngstown had a lot of infamous shootouts. There was the story of Flip Williams who executed four people. There was a murder over a video game. There was a race war in the junior high. There was a car chase and a shootout that led to an old Mexican woman being shot while watching a rerun of *Mash* in her living room. And last year there was a fire lit by a mentally retarded person that killed six people, the result of a dispute over a cell phone.

Frankie had participated in the shootout at a Youngstown high school. What it was about no one even remembered. It didn't matter. It wasn't over oil or conquest. It was high school kids who grew up poor badly rationalizing that shooting guns would lead to happiness. Frankie was caught in the crossfire. Someone dropped a gun on the cement, other people were shooting at him and his friends. He picked up the gun. He did not say, but one could assume that he cried and wet his pants in fear when he shot at the people who were shooting at him. He had never had the land to practice shooting a target so he fired in the general direction of the shooters out of fear and hit one of them in the leg. Frankie was arrested. The principal of the school testified that Frankie was shooting in self-defense. Frankie got one year in a juvenile detention center. When he got out his mother sent him to Dallas to live with relatives. Frankie lived down there staying out of trouble for several years. He graduated high school, went to parties, got jobs, and talked about the Cowboys. He came back. He was out with his cousin at a bar on the south side of Youngstown. A fight broke out and his cousin was shot in front of him. He said he was close to his cousin. They had grown up together playing on the same streets, going through the same tribulations. Then a year later he went into a bar and the man who he shot when he was in high school saw him. Followed him home back to his mom's small house on the south side of Youngstown. Frankie laughing, still drunk from the drinks at the bar, still happy from dancing, got of his car. A man yelled, Frankie looked and three bullets hit him. One in his stomach, one in his arm, and one in his leg. He said he couldn't feel it at first. But soon enough he knew he had been shot. He got in his car because he realized he had not died. He saw his cousin die of bullets, he knew that bullets could kill a man. He drove to the hospital bleeding from three holes in his body. He dragged his wounded body into Saint Elizabeth's Hospital. They asked him if he had health care, he said no, but they took him anyway. They saved Frankie to keep him living, to keep him washing dishes.

Frankie didn't snitch on the man who shot him. He didn't seek revenge either. He knew that the man who shot meant it. He wanted Frankie dead. To snitch would ensure his death.

Frankie lived in Warren in a small apartment with a short little girl who comforted him in the night and made him laugh. He had two kids with women he wasn't with. He had a lot of moments that would break most people, but he kept going.

I walked by him and Frankie said, "Look at this, look at this," holding his cell phone.

I looked at him with a curious expression.

He held up his cell phone and said, "Look."

I looked down and it was a sumo wrestler's ass.

"What the fuck is that Frankie?"

He laughed hysterically and said, "That's a man's ass." He laughed like a madman.

"That sure is."

Then he turned serious and said, "This white girl says she had my baby. She said they ran the DNA and used one of my past DNA tests and they say its mine."

"That's three babies, isn't it?"

"Yeah, I got too many babies as it is."

"Have you tried pulling out?"

He didn't recognize that comment and said, "It's my first white baby."

"I almost had a black baby."

"You did?"

"Yeah, but the umbilical cord killed it."

"Oh, I have three babies now. But I gotta talk to a lawyer about this DNA test."

"That sounds good. Bring in the lawyers."

I walked away and realized that he didn't tell me the child's sex or name.

I was outside smoking in a small shack where the potatoes and cleaning chemicals were stored. I sat on a box of potatoes. It was chilly and lightly snowing. Beth came out, sat on a box of potatoes and began to cry. Beth was always crying. She cried every day. She was from Geneva, up by Cleveland and was a poor white girl that never had anything. She never confessed what her childhood was like. She wasn't into sharing her life. She got pregnant when she was 17 and got married to the father because she was told it was the right thing to do. Her husband refused to do anything. He would sit on the couch everyday instead of changing diapers and doing the dishes. In the last nine years of marriage he had worked for a total two years. He went to trucking school, graduated, got a job and then quit in less than two months. Beth once said, "I never had a life." We were all talking about the bar and how much fun we had. How we were in college, learning, not caring about things like kids. How our lives were less hard than hers. And she said, "I never had a life."

We asked her why she won't go out drinking. She said she wasn't allowed because she became a whore when she got drunk. We told her that was normal for a woman to become a whore when they got drunk, and it was normal for a man's penis to not work when he got drunk.

She didn't respond to that. She kept scorning her life and her choices in her head, silently in despair over how things turned out.

I said to Beth, "What's wrong."

She looked at her feet with tears flowing from her eyes and said, "I asked for a divorce today."

"That's good."

"But we're supposed to stay together for the kids."

I considered a response and said, "My parents didn't love each other. It sucks in its own way knowing that your parents are living in the same building even though they hate each other. You'll end up teaching your kids that maintaining a failed relationship is a good thing."

"I'll have to pay for a lawyer and have a custody battle. It'll be so hard."

"Yeah, but imagine how hard it'll be if you have to live like that for the next 40 years."

She didn't want to consider either of those fates and said, "He won't do anything but sit on that couch and watch television. We've argued so many times. I've begged him to get up, I've cried so many times to get him to help me. But he won't. He won't help me."

She stood up, threw her cigarette at the cement and went in the building.

The servers of America are a pitiful bunch. Some were in college and it wasn't bad. They were just passing through. But a lot were trying to live off of tips. It was a degrading job.

It was the end of the night and I was mopping the floor. I had mopped many floors. I mopped floors at Wendy's, Taco Bell, a nursing home, and several other restaurants. I was 28 and still mopping floors. The world looks down on people that mop floors. I would be going to New York City the next week to a world full of people that didn't mop floors. It never bothered me to

34

mop floors though. I kind of liked it. I would look down at the floor before I would start and say to myself, 'Wow, what a dirty floor." Then I would mop it with industrial strength de-greaser and bleach. Then spray it off with a hose so it would look beautiful.

After we were done at the end of the night I went in the office and said to Renee, "We're done, can you check us out?"

"Oh, my god, whatever."

I left the office and stood in the kitchen. Diego stood near me staring at his shoes. Every night we had to get checked out. We COULD NOT LEAVE until we had been checked out by a manager. We were adults but we needed to checked out by another adult.

Renee came out and said, "Oh, you think you boys are done?"

Then she walked up the line and kept saying, "This is disgusting, this is so disgusting, don't you have any self-respect, don't you take any pride in your work."

We listened and wiped down the areas she designated.

It was the same thing every night. She would come out and say the same things about how everything was disgusting and how we needed to take pride in our work.

And every night we didn't care if it was disgusting or about taking pride in our work.

It never occurred to me how to take pride in cooking at a restaurant when I didn't own it, they didn't give good raises and didn't pay enough to afford the crappy health care they offered to their employees. None of the cooks had gotten a raise in a year since the hiring of the new head manager. Before we got raises every four months if we did a good job. And especially since the economy had recently collapsed raises were really out of the question. The only thing keeping us at that job was the fact that there were no other jobs. The area factories had recently sent out several 1000 workers into the labor pool that didn't mind working 50 hours a week and had kids to feed. The classifieds were empty, Craigslist was silent to our needs. The only thing that kept us there was the phrase, "At least I have a job."

But I liked the job. Or maybe I liked working. It gave me something to do. It was thoughtless. It was an escape. You went somewhere and did things you didn't care about. People told you what to do. You had a level of responsibility. If you performed their tasks the way they wanted them, they never cared. Without work I felt bored. I didn't really like work when I was younger. Taking shit and doing things I didn't want to do. But I got used to it after it awhile. One learns to suffer after awhile with stupid shit. I recognized this is what everybody does and what makes the world. People going to work, each doing their own little part, everyone agreeing that everybody else needs to find something to do. Each with their own little thing.

It was around that time that I noticed the strange relationship co-workers developed. My mother always mentioned it. She had worked at the Chevy plant for 33 years and always talked about how she watched her co-workers grow old. But what was strange to her, was that they didn't notice it happening. It was slow over the course of 30 years. Like time lapse photography. Watching each other slowly wrinkle up and droop.

I had worked at the steak house for two years and had already watched four women go through complete pregnancies. They even came in and I held their babies. I had attended birthday parties, cookouts, college graduation parties and a New Years bash with my co-workers. They had slowly become my friends. People I thought and even worried about. There were some I disliked at first, but eventually after spending 30 to 40 hours a week together, for years, they become like a sibling and you learn to put up with it.

6.

     I walked in the house, Amanda was sitting there pissed that I took so long. She was dressed in tight fitting clothes ready to get drunk and look sexy while dancing. Her make-up was on perfectly, her hair modeled into a messy yet organized formation on her head. She said, "Where you been, we gotta go."

     I thought, "What the fuck is the hurry," but instead said, "Okay, I'll hurry."

The response made her happy.

     I didn't feel like making her mad. Making her mad could make her cry. And making her cry was something I didn't want to deal with. It was better to choose to play along most of the time with people and their insanity. I had grown tired of arguing and crying and all the misery that goes along with conflict, so I threw my dirty work clothes off in silence and took a shower.

     When my father would come home from work it was the same every day. He would come in the house in silence. He wouldn't say hi or speak to anyone. He would shit. Every day he would shit when he got off of work, perfectly timed, it was amazing the accuracy of the time he would shit. Then he would leave the bathroom, go to the kitchen pick up a newspaper and carry it to his Lazy Boy chair. Hit the handle on the chair and lay back reading the paper. There was still no talking. No hello, no how are you, no how was school. He would read the paper for a little over 20 minutes and then fall asleep with the paper on his lap. He would wake up a half an hour later and do something. He would go outside and feed the rabbits and the chickens. Collect some brown eggs, bring them back to the house. Then mow the grass or weed whack. It was the same thing every day.

     My mother would come home around midnight and slam her car keys down on the kitchen table. She would talk endlessly to my father about her day at work. How it was a tragedy, how everyone was conspiring against her. How her back was killing her. How she had a sinus headache that wouldn't go away.

My father never even spoke back. He would play along and say nothing. She didn't require any responses.

When I got home from work, it was a shower, then I would check my email. Amanda and I might say some things to each other. But not much. It was a moderate amount of talking. Neither of us were silent nor babbling morons. We just said things when they needed to be said. As opposed to my mother who talked endlessly about nothing, and my father who needed to say things but refused to even say hello to his children.

Amanda and I arrived at the bar we go to every Sunday. It was down in Niles by where we work. It used to be an Italian restaurant but it closed and became a bar. It was the new hip bar on 422. All the restaurant workers on 422 were going to it. 422 was where the mall and all the restaurants were. There was Red Lobster, Outback, Olive Garden, Max and Erma's, Road House, and one called something like Fattie's in the mall. People who work at restaurants are notorious drunks. All the bars were full of us drinking ourselves stupid every night.

The bar was newly remodeled. It was shaped like a box with a low ceiling. There were tables, booths and chairs on both sides. A nice horseshoe bar in the middle. Three flat screen high-definition televisions hanging above the bar that played the highlights of the Steelers game. Young attractive bartenders that attended the local colleges who had bright futures and didn't consider bartending their destiny served the drinks.

The bar was new and shiny. It was unlike the other bars in the area. Youngstown had a lot of bars with cheap drinks. But the bars were old looking, not remodeled since the seventies. With high ceilings built in the 30s. There was too much history in those bars. Nobody was into history there that night. Everyone had cell phones, newer cars they were making payments on, new clothes from the mall, new hairstyles, everyone was singing new music. Everyone was really into the new.

Over half the people there were wearing Steelers jerseys and hats. The Steelers had won. People expected the Steelers to be good that year, but no one expected them to be that good. Everyone was getting drunk celebrating the victory of the Steelers. Libations were poured, sacrifices were made, everyone believing that through the purchasing and mass consumption of alcohol The Steeler Nation would appease the Football Gods and be granted more victories.

Everyone yelled when Amanda and I came in. She had her Red Lobster group and I had my Steak House group, both of our groups knew each other because we drank there every Sunday.

I looked around the bar to see who I knew and wanted to talk to first: There was The Big Smooth.

He was wearing a Steelers jersey and completely drunk. He was a big man. He was six four and 260 pounds. His hands were huge monsters at the end of his arms. He was daunting in size. But when you got to know him he was polite and sensitive. He read war books all the time, *The Naked and the Dead* and *Flags of our Fathers*. We would often trade books back and forth. We would sit on our smoke breaks from work or at a bar and discuss the books and the wars they were about.

The Big Smooth was kind of homeless then and living with friends. He was in his early 30s and his dad wouldn't stop yelling at him about drinking every night and not getting a good manly job that paid 40,000 a year and had benefits. His parents were hard working people that lived in a nice neighborhood, paid their bills and had enough money left over to buy things they didn't need. The Big Smooth only bought things he needed and lived simply. There are some people that don't need much, which contradicted many people's version of how people should behave. The Big Smooth held an old philosophy of living by what one needed, being friendly because courtesy made the best outcomes and created the most quiet, and simplicity because an excess of desire for objects and prestige led to an excess of responsibilities that people could actually live without. Of course it wasn't that simple. He had spent several nights in jail for fighting and had several DUIs. He could get out of hand. I had never seen him out of hand. He had always been peaceful in my company.

I went over to him, he gave me a big bear hug. Wrapped his large arms around me and said, "The Steelers won," then he hit the bar with his fist and yelled, "Go Steelers!"

He was drunk, slurring his words. He could barely move, he was clumsy.

Then he pointed at a random guy with nicely combed hair and said, "I threw a dart at that guy last time I was here."

"That guy over there."

"Yeah, that guy."

"What he do?" I said.

"He was pissing me off."

"What he do though?"

"His hair was pissing me off, it was so nicely combed."

"He puts gel in it," I said.

"What kind of man puts gel in his hair?"

39

"He looks like he shaves everyday."

"I can't drink whiskey. It makes me want to hurt people."

"Men want to fight when they're drunk and women want to fuck, that's what happens."

"Women become sluts when they're drunk."

"That's true."

Then Linda came over. She was a server from the steak house. She was a short, slightly pudgy girl with dark brown hair. I didn't really know her. She was a new hire and we had never really spoken. The only thing I knew about her was that she was very open. One day she talked about how she had a boyfriend and he would ask her to fuck him in the ass with a strap on all the time. She said they broke up eventually and she told people about it. The guy then got mad. She told him that if you want to do things like that, you better be prepared to have no shame. She didn't seem to have any hobbies or love anything but drinking and sex. She wasn't interested in life at all.

Linda yelled at me, "Where have you been all my life?"

She would always yell that at me and other men, I responded, "Waiting for you."

"Here I am baby."

She started touching my belly. I felt no sense of arousal from it.

She went over to The Big Smooth and started on him. I don't think he'd had a woman in a while and he was very receptive to it.

I went over to Sarah. Sarah was the queen of the steak house. She had been there for over six years. All her friends were steak house people. She had a long story. She grew up poor with a father that abandoned her. A mother that didn't really care. The dead beat father got sick, called her once on the phone and then died. Her brother ended up in prison for killing somebody. She got drunk one night and got pregnant by a man eight years older than her. They were going to get married but he eventually left and got married to somebody else. A daughter was born. Sarah grew to love the child. She had been going to college for seven years, had switched her major about twenty times. Had about five boyfriends in the last two years since the baby daddy left. Each relationship lasting about five months. After one would end, she would immediately start another. She wanted a daddy but had the complete inability to commit to a relationship because she was convinced that all men would eventually leave and break her heart. So she decided to start relationships and end them before they could end them. She had become a master of this game and everyone that knew her knew she was endlessly playing it. And we would watch one man after another enter into her life. We would stare at the new man knowing that at any time we would never see him again.

Sarah was leaning on the bar drunk as a human could get. All her words came out sluggish and blurred. Her movements were clumsy. Her eyes barely open. At times tears came from her them. She had just broken up with her fiance. She was planning to get married to a really good guy named Dave. Dave was a college educated man who worked helping juvenile substance abusers get back on track. On the weekends he would do carpentry with his dad to make extra money. He was a very responsible person. He finished school in less than five years, paid his bills on time, had good credit. He owned a newer motorcycle, had a newer car. He was nice. Always courteous and polite. He was what anyone would call "a nice guy." Dave tried to get Sarah to love him for over a year before she relented and started dating him. When they began dating, things went quickly. Dave moved in with Sarah and the kid. Dave was a sweetheart to the kid. The kid loved Dave. He would always play with her. He would take her out. He babysat and spent money on her without complaining. But Sarah didn't want that. Her father was irresponsible and shiftless. Her mother dated men of the same character. She knew the logical choice was Dave. Rational self-interest notified her that a responsible man was best for her and her child. But she was confused by responsibility. The shiftless male made sense to her. Women were supposed to love shiftless men. Men who lacked courage and self-control she viewed as optimal mates.

I stood next to her while she sat in a barstool, Sarah said, "I'm drunk."

"I can see that," I said.

"The Steelers won."

"Yes, life is good. You broke up with Dave, they said you fucked someone in the back seat of your car?"

"Yeah, in the back seat. I was drunk."

"Like you are now?"

"No, not so drunk."

"Dave was a good guy."

"I wasn't happy."

"Wasn't happy, he has money and an education."

"I wasn't happy. I'm drunk. Shut up."

"Are you crying?"

"You've seen me cry like 50 times, what makes this different."

"I guess it doesn't."

Then she hit me in the dick.

41

I bent over and held my dick.

"You punched me in the dick."

"That's true."

"You have issues."

"I'm so drunk."

I punched her in the arm really hard.

She said, "Oh, my god. I need a new boyfriend."

"Do you want a drink?"

"Okay."

I ordered a rum and coke.

She didn't say thank you, she put her drunken fingers around it. Then pulled it close to her face. Slowly put her mouth around the area of the straw. She was so drunk the straw went up her nose the first time. But then she was able to get the straw in her mouth. She slowly sipped the drink. Sarah had forgotten I was even there. So I walked away.

Monica ran up to me and gave me a hug. She was a skinny half-Italian girl that spent her days working at Red Lobster and her nights drinking herself stupid. She was another girl with no father and a heartless mother. Her hair was intensely gelled and looked like something out of *Moonstruck*.

I said, "Monica, your hair looks great."

"Oh, thank you. I worked really hard on it. Do you wanna see my cleavage, I have cleavage tonight."

"That sounds wonderful."

She pushed her little tits together and made cleavage.

"It makes me wanna put my tongue in it."

"You know you can't, I have Brandon down in Columbus."

"You and Brandon go well together, so I'll keep my tongue to myself."

She laughed not knowing I was being sarcastic about everything I said. She was completely convinced that her hair was great and her cleavage made me horny. She was attractive and it would not have been hard to have sex with her. But it didn't really matter to me. She lived alone in an apartment for the last two years. She was fond of farting and burping as loud as possible. She watched a lot of television and had no political opinions. She lived a lonely life.

I went over to the table where everyone was sitting. Amanda's new boyfriend was there. She always had a new boyfriend. This one was named Joseph. Like everyone she liked to have someone around that appreciated and loved her. My generation was consumed with serial monogamy. We went from one person to the next. Even if we had kids it didn't matter. The state was happy to take care of them now. We viewed our romantic relationships like little boys with baseball cards, television shows, and the owning of cars. We liked to meet someone new. We enjoyed learning about them. We enjoyed sharing our lives with them. Talking about childhoods, our parents, our siblings, little things that happened when we were seven. We enjoyed meeting people for the first time and that slow revealing of who we really are. It was all theatrical. Our sex was neurotic, with no intention of procreation. It always involved dirty talk, violence, paddles, handcuffs, anal sex, dildos, strap ons, and threesomes. There was no getting married and quietly walking as virgins into the bedroom on a wedding night awkwardly trying to have that first sex. Our awkward first sex was a distant memory, that we would laugh over, usually over the phone.

Joseph was a tall man. He grew up with a Christian preacher for a father in Hartford. A small country town 20 minutes by outside of Youngstown. He was one of those Christians that voted for Bush in 04 and in 08 voted for Obama. He had a bible in his car and knew it well. The pages were ruffled, there were little notations next to lines he felt were important. Several book markers were found amongst the pages. His father had made sure he learned the bible.

Several years ago, between the 04 and 08 election a change had occurred. What it was, he never said. But a realization that creationism, pro-life militancy, and the love of foreign wars had nothing in common with responsibility, kindness, and sincerity.

Joseph was wearing a bright blue shirt with a white tie and dress pants. He believed it was important to be drunk and well-dressed at the same time. His hair was gelled and styled. My hair was not combed. I couldn't comb my hair because of genetics. My father was Sicilian and had nappy hair. If I combed my hair it would turn into an afro. I had spent my life completely unable to comb my hair. It was a detriment to my everyday life. It was hard getting a job without properly combed hair. One could never be a server in a restaurant, a hedge funder, a school teacher, or anything that made above 12,000 a year without nicely gelled and styled hair. Joseph had a very good shot at life. He was a server and had learned how to speak Spanish. I believe pragmatically that if I had hair that could have been combed I would have been able to rise to levels of success undreamed up by the normal man. But my hair could not be combed. It was my tragic flaw. Like Oedipus having sex with his mother. But for me it was my hair. I couldn't even be a proper hipster with curly hair. Male hipsters had brown hair that flowed nicely over their head. That went over their

43

forehead and looked appealing to the eye. I had come into luck though. Michael Cera, an actor, a man who played in movies being ironic was also half-Sicilian and had hair that could not be combed. It looked combed but I knew it wasn't. He was just pushing it down with his fingers. Perhaps he had stylists with specially built combs for people who were half-Sicilian mixed with Northern European white people. Women started finding my hair attractive.

Joseph's hair daunted me. I was a writer. I wasn't really a writer. I had not made enough money to live as a writer and call myself a writer. My parents ingrained in my being so deep that it is part of my Self that a person cannot call themselves something unless they are making money doing it. If a person golfs on the weekend. They like to golf. They are not a golfer. Tiger Woods was a golfer, not Bob the shift manager at Denny's. If you acted in cheap horror movies on Thursday and you could not pay your car insurance with cheap horror movies then you were not an actor.

Joseph yelled, he was always very excited, "How was work?"

It occurred to me say it was bleak but I said, "It wasn't memorable."

He laughed and said, "We're all going to Monica's after the bar closes and playing Monopoly."

Monopoly was a game with a little metal shoe.

"I have to get up early and get on a bus."

"We'll get you there."

Amanda heard and said, "He's always nervous about getting to places on time."

"It is important to be on time." I'm always on time because I know my hair looks terrible.

"We'll get you there on time."

"I'm going to get really drunk."

"That's cool. This is a bar."

"I suppose this is the place where a person can get drunk."

"Can't do it at a cell phone store."

"No, this is the place."

I went to the bar to get another drink, the bartender came over. His name was Tom. Tom dated Sarah for awhile. It was a six month pointless relationship. They fought all the time and were jealous of each other. Sarah had to text message Tom every hour or Tom would get worried that Sarah was fucking somebody else. Sarah even bought a special cellphone with a keypad so she could type quicker to Tom.

Tom came over and said, "Hey, how's it going?"

"Life is awesome, Captain and coke."

Then Tom said with a serious face. Tom always had a serious face. He considered everything he said to be serious, essential and vital. Tom said, "I didn't hit her."

"You didn't what."

"Hit her. She broke three of my fingers."

Sarah was on the other side of the bar almost passed out sipping on a drink while he spoke

"How did she break your fingers?" I said.

"She slammed them in a car door."

"That must have hurt."

"Yeah, it fucking hurt. There was fucking blood everywhere. I was drunk and bleeding everywhere. She kept yelling like a fucking retard. I kept yelling back at her with blood pouring out of my fingers. Then she started pushing me. Then she started punching me. I couldn't do anything to get her to stop."

It occurred to me he could have ran away. He could have realized she was a crazy bitch and gone home.

Tom went on, "So I pushed her. I was like, 'fuck this.' And pushed her back. It wasn't like I was trying to beat up a woman. Then she called the police."

"I heard the police got called."

"Yeah, she fucking called the police. The police showed up and of course took her side of the story. I had to spent a night in jail. I had to hire a lawyer and go to court for assault and battery. I had to spend a thousand fucking dollars for all that shit."

"What the court decide?"

"The lawyer showed pictures of my broken fingers and showed the hospital records. And they dropped the charges. But what the fuck is that? She brought me to court for pushing her."

"She never mentioned breaking your fingers."

"Of course she didn't. She also said that all you guys hated me for being a violent woman-beater."

"I never hated you."

I honestly couldn't remember ever thinking about him. But I doubt he cared about hearing that.

Tom looked stressed out, like he was in Iraq and had to enter the house of a known insurgent and kill everybody in the house before they killed him. I wasn't sure what he was so stressed about.

Tom said, "Look at her now, all drunk. Broken up with another guy. I'm happy about it. She deserves her life. She's alone over there, drunk, and no one cares. It is so predictable."

"The desire for self-destruction is stronger in some."

"Yeah, that's what I'm saying. She's self-destructive. She doesn't care who gets in the way. She builds up her life. Then destroys it."

"She's bored. There isn't anything to do here."

"I don't know why she does it. Everybody has their problems."

"True that."

"I gotta get back to work. I just wanted to find out if you hated me."

"No, I don't hate you Tom."

Tom went back to work. I stood at the bar drinking my Captain and coke. Tom, like Sarah, was a person with a dead father. It was always the same stories. These patriarchs who had left, these patriarchs who didn't love, and these patriarchs who died. Western civilization was dominated by these patriarchal influences. There was God and Jesus, Mars and Romulus, Mohammad and Fatima, George Herbert Walker Bush and George W. Bush and finally God The Father. Our fathers weren't much. They would come home from work and take naps. They would bring us to a baseball game and not talk to us while we were there. Sometimes they would beat us for being annoying. Over half of my generation's fathers had left them with their bitter mothers. It wasn't terrible. We were Americans and had food, air-conditioning, and indoor plumbing. But people for whatever reason like to have their fathers around. And they like their fathers not to be jackasses. Which was a problem because consumerist attention deficit disorder based societies produce in mass jackasses. But we still like our jackasses to be around. Tom and Sarah's jackasses died. Neither of their fathers were around and then they died. They were reared by sad bitter women who never remarried but had a thousand boyfriends over their lives. Women who constantly showed a sense of disdain for the opposite sex who left them to die with their children.

Went up to a girl that Amanda worked with named Marissa. Marissa was a small white girl that looked like she was from northern Europe. Like she was from a tribe that herded Reindeer. I wanted to call her Ingrid or Olga.

I went up to her and yelled, "Marissa!"

"Hey, what's going on?"

"I feel very happy right now."

"That's good. So am I. I'm drunk."

"Good, we are equals then."

"Yes, unity through alcohol," Marissa said excitedly.

"Are you looking for romance?"

"You are so silly."

"No, I'm serious. Romance. Like in a Jennifer Aniston movie. I'll be that guy you know that isn't perfect but can be fixed. And you can fix me. Don't you want to fix me."

"I do enjoy fixing men."

"I'm a total fixer upper. I need a good woman to make me right. To make me into a man. To make this pile of human waste to a functional adult that produces and feeds his babies."

"I've only met you twice."

"Twice is enough for love. Doesn't anybody believe in love at first sight anymore? This would be love at third sight. But still it would be love. And the production of babies."

"I haven't considered reproduction. I just graduated from college."

"That's perfect. Now that you've graduated you can reproduce. I'll work at Indelex and you can stay home and watch the babies."

"They just closed Indelex."

"I'll work at Craftmaid."

"They laid off everybody there."

"Goddamn woman, how are we supposed to reproduce and carry on the human species if there are no jobs?"

"I don't know."

"People without jobs have babies all the time."

"I don't wanna raise my babies on welfare," said Marissa.

"You're right. What degree did you get anyway?"

"Criminal justice."

"Oh, that's a good one. You can become a detective. You can be like those people on *Law and Order*."

"I don't know, I'm not a very dominant person."

"You can shoot people. That would be awesome. You can scream at them things like, 'I know you did it, you child-fucking bastard!' And then punch them in the cock. Imagine it. That would be so fucking sweet. And you have the certificate that allows a person to do that."

"I know. That does sound fucking awesome."

"Seriously. You could be out there shooting the bad guys, sticking them in jail. All kinds of crazy fun adventures a person with a criminal justice degree can have."

"I was thinking of working for Homeland Security. I would protect us from terrorists."

The word "terrorists" flashed through my drunken brain. It sent Dick Cheney and Bush's face to the forefront of my brain. I could see Dick Cheney and Bush's face saying things about evil, danger, horror, mass murder, chemical, biological, Hitler, Saddam, all of that shit flashed through my mind. All that crazy shit that crazy bastard said to this crazy country. All those beautiful Platonic Noble Lies that fucker told us to get Iraqi oil so we could drive our cars, make cell phones, computers and garbage cans out of petroleum.

I said, "You're going to catch terrorists?"

"Yeah, terrorists. Doesn't that sound exciting. I wouldn't personally. I would work in intelligence helping to track them down. Maybe working for the Pentagon."

More images flew through my head, of Abbie Hoffman and Norman Mailer circling the Pentagon trying to elevate it. Then of the thing on fire, burning. I had seriously never met anyone in my life that wanted to work in the Pentagon.

"Obama is president now. He's going to make friends with the terrorists and we are all going to be in love and have sex and cake."

"No, Obama hates the terrorists. He always says we are going to 'defeat you.'" She said "defeat you" in a very serious tone while pointing her index finger at my chest.

"You're right. He does want to attack Pakistan."

"Yeah, he's going to need intelligence for that. And I want it to be me."

"Does that job pay well?"

"Yeah, probably."

"Does it offer good health care and a 401K?"

"I'm sure they offer health care, but I think the government supplies a pension. Which is better than a 401k. My mom's 401k is gone."

"Gone?"

"Yeah, she came home yesterday after work crying and said it was all gone."

"What's her plan?"

"She doesn't have one. She just sat in the kitchen and cried."

"What did you do?"

"I didn't do anything. It made me feel confused. Like what is the point? A person works for years and sees their retirement disappear. She's like 55. She doesn't have enough working years left to make it back."

"Your parents are divorced?"

"Yeah, my dad left when I was nine. He just moved across town though. I did that two-weekends-a-month thing."

Monica came running over and yelled at us, "Monopoly at my house after."

Marissa screamed, "FUCK YEAH! MONOPOLY!"

I was terrified of Monopoly and said, "Fuck yeah," in a sad pathetic drunken voice.

Monica continued, "Yeah, everyone is excited. Joseph is pumped. He wants to be the shoe."

Marissa yelled with a high degree of madness, "I want the hat. I always win with the hat."

Monica looked at me and said, "What piece are you gonna play with?"

"Hmm, the dog."

Marissa yelled, "Oh my god, you want to be the dog. Nobody ever wins with the dog."

"I feel that this is the dog's lucky night," I said.

Monica yelled, "No, the dog is never lucky. You're doomed with the dog. You should be the hat."

"I don't wanna be a hat. A hat isn't even alive. I want to be an organism."

"You need to take this seriously, Monopoly isn't a joke," said Marissa.

Monica said, "Yeah, how you play Monopoly shows what kind of man you are. Like if you can take control in bed and show a woman what it means to be a woman."

"Are you serious?" I said.

"Oh yeah, it's all about competition. About how you can take down your fellow humans, destroy them in front of their friends and lovers. They are so embarrassed when they have been destroyed. I love to destroy my opponents. I want them to cry themselves to sleep after I have annihilated them. I know when I see a man work hard to beat out his friends playing Monopoly I know that guy is good in bed. Because he wants to win that orgasm. He strives to make that woman have the best orgasm she ever had. So she'll never forget it. She walk her days always remembering that orgasm he gave her. She will hate all men that cannot give her that orgasm," said Marissa.

"I've never thought it about like that," I said.

Marissa continued, "You should. It's the same for women. Women who want to win at monopoly want to give their boyfriends huge orgasms. That's

49

what Monopoly is about."

"Sex?"

"Oh yeah. It is like an orgy of sexual tension," said Marissa.

Monica started to have a funny look on her because she was also confused about what drunken Marissa was talking about. Monica said, "I'm gonna go talk to Amanda."

Marissa said, "That's why I voted for Barack Obama. He's all competition all the time. You can tell that Obama fucks with determination to be the best fuck that woman ever had. That man competes constantly. He is truly American. He loves to destroy his opponents. Did you see him destroy Hillary. I mean, I'm a woman, but I don't really like them. But I do like men that seem like they have sex like they mean it. He seems like he would have sex with a sense of charity too. Like if Barack Obama was going down on me, and he didn't want to anymore, maybe because his jaw hurt or something. Barack Obama would suffer through it and keep eating that pussy until an orgasm blossomed."

"Blossomed?"

"Oh yeah, the female orgasm blossoms, it arises from the earth like flowers on the apple trees in the spring."

"I thought it blew up like a grenade."

"No, blossom. But listen, Barack Obama destroys. He went up to McCain at those debates and annihilated him. I didn't know who to vote for, but when I saw him just wreak havoc upon John McCain in those debates and McCain walking creeping around the stage at that town hall meeting, saying all that crazy shit about the KGB. I knew he loved to destroy his opponents. And that's what makes a great president. He wants to be the best president. He looks at paintings of Abe Lincoln and says, 'Bitch, you know who I am. I'm gonna take your ass down.' Then he flicks off the painting and swaggers down the hallways the White House."

"That sounds like really weird behavior," I said.

"No, it isn't. That's totally normal for competitive people."

"John Kennedy was competitive and he almost caused a nuclear war."

"Hmm, America is about competition. It is about the individual expression of destroying your opponent. We can't all be writers. Some of us express ourselves through games."

"Okay, I get it."

Marissa screamed, "Obama will beat them all."

Then the lights came on and the bar was closed. It always sucked when the lights came on. You knew it was over then. No more drinks. No more bar fun. The music was over. Everyone would disperse like nothing ever happened. Everyone put on their coats. Their stocking caps and gloves. The night was over. People went to the bar and paid their tabs with credit cards. Why people thought it would be prudent to buy alcohol with credit cards I never figured out. But they did and didn't care what the consequences were.

For some reason Tom was crying. Amanda and I went over. Tom was washing glasses and said, "My dad died two years ago and Christmas season is driving me crazy. I don't know what is wrong with me. I've been thinking about it all night."

We stared at him and said nothing.

Then we looked and Monica was crying. She was text messaging her boyfriend in Columbus and tears were going down her cheeks. Tears tumbled over her freckles down into her mouth. She grabbed one of those small napkins off the bar and blew her nose. We knew why she was crying and didn't ask, but she supplied the information anyway, "I'm so sad. I miss Brandon so much. He's down there all alone sitting in his parent's house. I want to be with him. I would really feel good if I was with him."

We didn't say anything.

Everyone was crying.

Several people were helping Sarah get to the door. She was so drunk she couldn't even walk. It looked like she was crying too. Hopefully she wasn't planning on driving. Maybe she would drive. People do that. They get in their cars drunk to the point of having the mental state of a tree and drive their cars into telephone poles. The pole gets bent a little, their car is destroyed and they get a DUI and have to pay 2,000 in legal fees. And then the state sends them a letter stating they have to pay for the telephone pole which is another 1,000. Then they have to go to DUI camp in Austintown for the weekend where they talk about their feelings. Then they don't drink for a week telling everyone they are "turning over a new leaf." Everyone tells them that's great. Then a week later you see them in a bar drunk, but they have no license for a year so they have to walk home. Then you see them walking down the street drunk at night and instead of offering them a ride you just laugh and beep. And that is what is called life. What separates man from the animals? Animals cannot get DUIs.

7.

I ended up in a car.

In the backseat with Monica.

I was drunk.

Monica looked beautiful.

She had stopped crying.

Her make-up ran a little down her cheeks.

I love when black make-up runs down a woman's cheeks.

When she looks all torn and true.

She put her hand on my leg.

Joseph was up front driving.

Amanda was beside him touching his cock.

Monica was jealous and moved closer to me.

I moved closer to Monica.

I said, "I don't know if I can fuck tonight. I'm so drunk. It might not work."

Monica laughed.

Then Joseph hit a curb.

The car shook violently.

"HOLY SHIT," Amanda yelled.

Monica was laughing hysterically.

I yelled, "I can't die tonight, I'm supposed to get on a bus in the morning."

"Where are you going?" Monica said in a sluggish voice.

"I'm going to NYC, bitches. I'm getting interviewed."

"What magazine?"

"Fuck, if I know. They want to talk to me and other writers about shit. What shit, who knows."

It was dark in the backseat. It always weirded me out how we rode in darkness in cars. Especially when I was drunk. Riding along the street in public in the darkness. Engulfed in darkness like we were in the jungle, going to sleep, or fucking.

Joseph yelled back, "I'm sorry guys. I won't hit anymore curbs."

"Please don't, I must get on a bus."

Amanda yelled at me, "Calm down, we'll get you on that fucking bus."

"I don't believe you. You're never on time for anything."

"Don't judge me when I'm drunk."

"I'm not judging you, I'm stating facts. Judging is like saying you're a bad person."

"No, you're judging. I feel judged."

Joseph yelled, "Judge not, lest he be judged."

Amanda said, "Did you hear that, don't judge."

"I'm not judging, I'm stating empirical evidence on why I'm worried that I won't be there. I'm so drunk."

Monica rubbed my hair with her little half-Italian hand and said, "Don't worry. They'll get you there. Calm down."

"I believe you, whatever. Have we started playing Monopoly yet?"

We pulled into Monica's driveway. She lived in a house that was divided up into three apartments. When the steel mills closed there were 500 thousand people living in the area. 300 thousand left. It left a lot of big nice houses. Slum lords bought them in the 80s and converted them into apartments. Monica lived in one.

We went into the apartment. It was a sad little place. It had white walls painted with the cheapest paint possible. There were a couple of couches that she got from relatives for free or maybe from a thrift store. A small television. A kitchen that hadn't been remodeled since the 80s. And a bedroom with a nice double bed. I walked around the apartment imagining her sleeping alone at night. Nobody around to hold her. Monica would wake up and go piss alone. She would sing country music to herself when she was pissing in the early morning. Then she would go to the kitchen and cry singing country music making herself scrambled eggs with bacon. She didn't drink coffee. She would drink orange juice bought from the dollar store. She would sit at her kitchen table text messaging her love in Columbus and eating scrambled eggs. Her mother would call. She hated answering her mother's number but she would anyway because she would feel guilty if she didn't. Her mother would bitch at her about things that didn't matter and had no relevance to anyone's life. Monica would listen and bitch back. She would tell her mother she was going to take a shower and hang up. She wouldn't take a shower. She went to the living room. Laid down on one of the used couches and watched television.

I laid on Monica's bed and Monica laid next to me. Amanda was sitting on the edge of the bed. Then Monica got on top of me. I put my hands on her thighs. She giggled and laughed. Then kissed Amanda. They made out. Their tongues in each other's mouths. They always kissed when they were drunk. I knew very few women that did not show bisexual behavior. Pretty much every woman I knew would make out with a girl when she was drunk. No one considered that homosexuality. No one mentioned it as anything sociological. It was just what women were like now. They were bisexual. Of course a lot of men would give each other blow jobs in porn stores and truck stops. The mainstream media never mentioned all the homosexuality taking place. It was obvious to everyone that America had become a bisexual nation. But America still wanted to pretend that everyone was living in beautiful houses having nice straight sex getting married and having children that would one day grow up to use crystal meth or go to Harvard.

I looked up at Monica and said, "I like you on top of me."

Monica giggled.

Marissa arrived and so did the bartender Tom.

Monica jumped off me. I watched her walk away from me. She didn't want anyone thinking she was cheating on her boyfriend. She knew that everyone loved drama and somebody would email her boyfriend down in Columbus. She had already got in trouble for cheating on her boyfriend with a guy named Buddy. Buddy was a small man. He was five foot five inches tall. He weighed 130 pounds and was covered in really dumb tattoos. Things like dragons, snakes, and skulls spitting fire. Brandon found out of course and punched a hole in the wall. The hole was still there. I looked at it and giggled to my drunken self. Her boyfriend of course broke up with her. They weren't swingers. They were people that liked to play ownership games. Having a relationship creates a game. A court with rules, regulations, and privileges. And one of those regulations is no cheating. But she got drunk and cheated. She knew better. But she wanted drama. Her parents were divorced and she was afraid of commitment. Her boyfriend left and went back to Columbus. Monica was left to eat scrambled eggs alone. She called him when he was down in Columbus and fell in love again. Why he would expect her to stay faithful I didn't know.

Tom had stopped crying. But he did seem emotionally disenfranchised. Tom was a sad person. Sarah said he was bipolar. I personally had never seen him walking around happy and perky. If he was ever manic it never happened around me.

Marissa was drunk. But she was sober enough to play Monopoly. Everyone was excited about Monopoly. They kept talking about past games of Monopoly. Who beat who and how they beat them. Everyone had a philosophy on Monopoly. I had never played Monopoly. I was scared.

The board was put out on the floor. Everyone gathered around the board like Navajos in a sweat lodge. Like students gathered around Socrates and disciples gathered around Jesus. They herded together in a little group, with pagan idols as game pieces to match wits. To own spaces on a board. To play capitalist. To become the owners of large corporations determined to reap profits by searching the earth for the cheapest labor possible. They purchased real estate charging high rents, finding poor folk to share crop their land. Sending slave ships to Africa to pick their cotton. Sending boats to Southern Italy and Greece to work in their steel mills. Building a shoe factory in China, a shirt factory in Brazil. It was The Dream. And they were living it.

I was presented the dog piece. I looked down at the dog piece and felt wary. I was drunk. Too drunk to play Monopoly. Too drunk to care about a dog piece.

We started playing.

Marissa and Joseph were Monopoly Nazis.

They had very serious expressions of determination and capitalistic ambition.

Couldn't handle all that ambition and left the room without saying anything.

Walked into Monica's room.

Saw her bed.

It looked soft and polite.

I laid down.

The room was dark and everyone was yelling and screaming in the other room.

Monica came in and said, "You okay?"

"Your bed is nice."

"Do you want any McDonalds? Tom is going."

"No thank you. Tell Amanda we need to get up early and get on that bus. I'm going to NYC."

"Okay, whatever. I'll tell her."

8.

I woke up.

Looked around.

I was in a room I could not identify immediately.

It was Monica's room.

I looked around the bed and wondered where Monica was. I was hoping I would wake up next to Monica's cute little body. But she chose to sleep somewhere else in the apartment.

I was still drunk.

Then I realized I needed to get on a bus in downtown Youngstown.

I went to the bathroom and pissed.

Then went to the living room and saw bodies sprawled everywhere under cheap blankets.

Surveyed the room to find Amanda and Joseph.

I needed a cigarette. So I picked up Monica's pack of Newports off the coffee table and stole two of hers. I lit one. The cigarette made me feel better.

I tapped Joseph on the shoulder till he woke up. He didn't seem happy about having to get up. But he was a responsible person and Protestant so he stood up without complaint.

I kicked Amanda to wake up. She was pissed. She wasn't as Protestant as Joseph. Waking up was hard for her.

Monica yelled from underneath a blanket, "What the fuck are you doing? It's like 7 in the morning?"

"I need to get on a bus."

Joseph and Amanda got their shoes on and we left.

We had to drive back to the bar and get Amanda's car.

We pulled into the parking lot. The Big Smooth's SUV was still there.

I ran over to the SUV and looked in the window. The Big Smooth was sleeping under a thin blanket in the backseat. It was only 30 degrees outside. I thought about knocking on the window and waking him up so he could get to somewhere warm. But he was The Big Smooth and if anyone could sleep in freezing cold weather under a thin blanket it was him.

I ran to Amanda's car and we went home.

9.

Amanda drove me to the downtown Youngstown bus station. The bus station was located at the end of 193. A long road that started at the edge of Lake Erie and ended in downtown Youngstown. I grew up on 193 in Vienna. I've had five jobs on 193. My black baby that was strangled by his umbilical cord lied buried on 193. And I was even born on 193. And then I was going to take my trip to NYC from the end of 193. Someday they would take me back to that hospital I was born on 193 and I would die. Then they would bury me on 193 and my epigraph would say:

Born on 193
Lived on 193
Died on 193
Here he rests on 193

There will be no procession on 193. There will be no statues celebrating my presence on 193. There won't be any streets named after me. A lot of men and women were born, lived, worked and died on 193.

The bus station was full of poor black people. Old black men sitting alone in silence. Old black men in groups talking about the economy. Black women wearing cheap thrift store clothes holding babies talking on their cell phones. An upper class looking white guy was standing beside his bags. He had luggage. No one had luggage. Everyone had a bag, some had garbage bags. The white man with the nice haircut was talking on an I-phone standing next to his expensive luggage.

Got my ticket and Amanda and I went to the coffee shop. There were a lot of older white, Italian, and black men in there. They were sitting around talking chewing on donuts and sipping coffee. The coffee shop had a lottery machine. The older people would get the lottery tickets, scratch them and talk about their past big wins. It was nice to sit there seeing the old white, Italian, and black men sit together and reminisce about the steel mills.

I went to the bathroom at the back of the bus station. The bathroom was full of graffiti. The toilet didn't have a door. There were gang symbols everywhere. There were random quotes about Tupac and Biggie. There were three guys standing around talking about exchanging drugs at eight in the morning.

Walked out of the bathroom. Four young black guys and a young white guy dressed in baggy clothes and tilted baseball caps were rap battling. One would take turns insulting the other one. Everybody would laugh when something funny was said. A huge black security guard came in and starting yelling at them, "What the fuck do you think you're doing? Is this a concert hall? Does this look like a concert hall? I repeat does this look like a concert hall? Are there any tickets being sold? I don't see a stage. Do you see a stage?"

They answered, "What's your problem man?"

"I don't have a problem. I have hoodlums serenading each other in my bus station. What is your problem? This is a family institution. Nobody wants to hear you swear at each other. What is this? Tell me, is this a concert hall?"

"No," one replied in an angry voice.

"Don't you have a place to go, somewhere else you can serenade each other?"

They stood there looking angry.

"Do you understand what I'm saying, I'm saying this isn't a concert hall."

He kept repeating it, he kept yelling. He was very fervent.

The guys dispersed.

The security guard walked back up front swearing to himself about hoodlums.

There are a lot of hoodlums in Youngstown. Young black and white men who didn't graduate high school or barely did anything but stumble around Youngstown doing drugs, going to jail, prison, and impregnating women. White collar America did not enjoy those people, the hoodlums. They disgraced The American Dream of hard work and being ambitious. I didn't care, I had met many hoodlums over the years. They had shitty lives. They grew up in projects with crack head mothers most likely with no father figure except for the random men their mothers would fuck. They went to crowded schools and grew up without land to play on, without the comforts of the suburbs. They eventually grew out of it. They eventually stopped singing in bus stations and pulled their pants up and got jobs like everybody else. Hoodlums didn't cause the Afghan and Iraq Wars, they didn't cause the DOW to drop four thousand points.

Amanda and I went outside so I could smoke. Amanda didn't smoke.

Both of her parents smoked but she didn't out of protest. I enjoyed smoking. It relieved stress. It made me feel better. It gave my hands something to do. I wasn't concerned with living to 100. I wasn't concerned with my death at all. Death seemed like the least of my problems. I had a lot of problems, had a shitty car, had bills to pay, had a shitty job, never felt like I belonged anywhere. I don't know if feeling like one belongs anywhere constitutes itself as a problem but it was a problem for me. Smoking helped with that. I felt like I was a smoker. I was part of a great legion of those who smoked cigarettes and lived unhealthy lives.

The sky was overcast. It was a dreary day. Young and old black men stood around smoking laughing about girls with nice asses. Nobody was taking anything seriously. It was too early in the day for that.

Amanda said to me, "Are you coming back?"

"Coming back where?"

"Here."

"Of course I'm coming back."

"I'm worried you won't."

"I don't know what I would do there."

"You might not come back."

"I don't have enough money to leave."

"You have friends though, they might get you a job."

"No, I'll return. I have to finish school."

"I'll miss you."

"You'll have Joseph," I said.

"But I can't talk to him like I do you."

"I'll come back. This is where I live."

"Do you think you can live here forever?"

"I don't know. Do you think you can live here forever?"

"I don't know. I've been here forever."

"I'll return, you'll be picking me up soon enough."

"I don't like to sleep in the house alone."

We went back in and waited for the bus. I waited in a line. Amanda stood with me. The security guard called the people going to Pittsburgh to get on. We moved slowly in a nice line. I didn't have a suitcase. Just a book bag. I didn't even bring a change of clothes. I knew I would get off the bus at Times Square and didn't want to carry luggage for miles.

It was raining.

I hugged Amanda.

She looked sad.

I didn't know how to look, so I went with what she was doing and looked sad myself.

We let go of each other. I walked toward the bus and looked back at her, smiled. Trying to reassure her that I would return.

She smiled back.

I got on the bus.

I walked to the back of the bus and sat in the closest unoccupied seat to the bathroom.

Best Behavior

illustration by Ellen Kennedy

Best Behavior

10.

I closed my eyes. They were hungover and tired. I fell asleep and woke up in Pittsburgh.

I entered the Pittsburgh bus station. Every time I had been to the Pittsburgh bus station it was a different one. It was new and shiny. Americans love new and shiny. When something gets old and spray-painted, the bathrooms have too many cocks drawn on the walls. The sinks look a little aged. They don't paint over it. They don't remodel it a little. They send in bulldozers to demolish it. When it came to public works, it occurred to someone one day that demolishing and rebuilding something from scratch created more jobs than remolding. So America decided if a public building was even a little run down, instead of fixing it up, build a new one. It was logical.

The bus station was nice. It had good lighting. Not too bright, not too dark. I went to the bathroom and the walls of the stalls were made of metal so no one could write on them and they could wash easily. From every corner of America, from Maine, to Florida, New York to California, Americans love to write on bathroom stall walls. Men love to draw cocks. I've shit in bathrooms in Nebraska, Oregon, and Georgia. Every bathroom stall in America has a penis drawn on the wall. There was always a comment about how much somebody loved to suck cock. Usually there was one or two racial slurs and that old Homeric poem, "Here I sit broken hearted, come to shit and only farted." There were some people that didn't consider literature on bathroom stalls to be classy. So a lot of new bathrooms had metal walls.

I left the bathroom and went outside to smoke. I went out the front door, it was nowhere. I didn't know Pittsburgh well. I didn't know where I was. I knew there were several rivers somewhere in Pittsburgh, but where I didn't know. Everyone walking by had Steelers coats on. There was no ashtray outside of the gas station. Society fought a war against smokers and won. Instead of putting our cigarettes in ashtrays we put them on the sidewalk. It was a strange victory they had won.

Went to the food court. It was pathetic. A little black man in his 40s was making cheeseburgers by himself while talking on his cell phone. Everyone was on their cell phone. It didn't matter what color, what age, what gender, they were on their cell phones. Who they were talking to I didn't know. What they were talking about I didn't know. They were talking though. If they weren't talking they were text messaging. I grew up without cell phones. All the people I knew and myself didn't starve to death because we didn't have a cell phone. We had friends. People were able to get married and have kids. People had jobs. I looked around the food court and four people were talking on their cell phones and two were text messaging. Who were these people I thought. What did they need to say? Did they even talk to those people they were talking to in person? Does anybody want to talk to anyone in person anymore? Does anyone fuck in person or just talk on their cell phone?

A young journalist once told me while walking across campus that people had cell phones to be perceived as important. That they were so important, integral, essential to the functioning of society that people called them all the time and they needed to respond to that call because if they didn't civilization would collapse and humanity would be plunged into the *state of nature*. The state of affairs would cease, hospitals would crumble to the ground, roads wouldn't be repaired, the police would go on an endless lunch break, Saddam Hussein would be resurrected and put back in power, martial law would be declared, the constitution suspended, little children would disobey their mothers, boyfriends and husbands would instantly cheat on their girlfriends and wives, gay people would become straight, the straight gay, mayonnaise would start tasting like mustard, abortion would become illegal, and history would end in a whimper because they didn't answer their cell phone call and talk loudly in a public place.

A cute Asian woman in her late 20s stood next to me waiting for cheeseburgers. We looked at each other and then at the cheeseburgers and the little black guy talking on his cell phone. We couldn't speak the same language but our looks were enough, they said, "These cheeseburgers are gonna taste like shit."

I brought my cheeseburger to a table. It somewhat tasted like a cheeseburger. I wasn't sure when the cow was killed, where it was killed, what kind of cow it was, what the cow ate, but I was sure it was killed a long fucking time ago, it was probably a miserable cow, and the cow ate bad tasting grass that had little nutrition.

I imagined a miserable cow standing out in a field in Brazil alone. It was probably two years ago. The cow was chewing on some bad tasting grass. Looked around not caring about anything. Doing what cows have always done, ate grass and drank water. Then it was killed one day and its sirloin was ground up, stuffed in plastic bags, frozen and sent to America. Eventually it made it to a bus station in Pittsburgh.

I got in line for the bus. It was a terrible looking series of humans. Many were missing teeth, the men were bald, the women looked older than they were, kids were everywhere. Their clothes were bought from thrift stores. Their shoes had holes in them and they didn't smell good. It wasn't a collection of well-educated-well-balanced-well-rounded individuals. Fate had not done them well. They were the kind of people one imagines Jesus spoke to when he gave The Sermon on the Mount. Jesus walked up there and looked upon 1,000 suffering Jews wearing torn clothes holding their babies in their arms, men tired from work, a nation stifled by Roman imperialism. Their faces dirty missing teeth, trying to forget the past, tired of the present and terrified of the future.

The bus driver called us on the bus. There was still seven hours to go, seven long hours.

I found a seat in the back again.

In the back there were two white women, one in her twenties and one in her forties. The one in her twenties sat with a tall black guy in his twenties. They didn't have headphones or a book to read. The woman in her twenties whispered to the man in the backseat.

A black man in his late twenties dressed in baggy clothing talked on his cell phone.

I sat on the bus for an hour in silence listening to music on my headphones when the woman in her forties said, "Hey?"

I didn't respond at first and then she repeated it, "Hey, you!"

I looked over and said, "Yeah."

Her face was tired. Her skin was pale and ghostlike. Her hair looked dirty, it was brown and straight. Her body had a little fat on it but not too much. She wasn't attractive. She was more of those people that Jesus talked to on The Mount. Those miserable people that walk the earth in unhappiness. Not knowing what happiness is, happiness not even occurring to them as an option.

She said, "Her and I just got out of prison."

"How long were you in?"

"Four years."

"That's a long time."

"I know sweety, it is. That guy my girlfriend is sitting with just asked her to have sex with him. He just got out of prison too. We're all riding home together on the bus."

"I wasn't in prison."

"Where were you?"

"Youngstown."

"I'm from Allentown, that's like the same place."

"We both have songs."

"Yeah, yeah sweety. Billy Joel wrote ours, who wrote yours?"

"Bruce Springsteen."

"I think I heard that in a bar once," she said.

"It's a good song."

"Have you ever been to Allentown?"

"No."

"I think I drove through Youngstown once. But I can't remember."

"There's no reason for you to remember it."

"Yeah, ain't like its Disney Land."

"No, Youngstown isn't Disney Land and Allentown isn't Epcot Center," I said.

"Where you going?"

"New York City."

"What you doing there? Going to the Statue of Liberty, seeing a play on Broadway?"

"I'm bored." I could have said I was a writer, I was going to get interviewed by a magazine, but I doubted she cared. I doubted I even cared. Boredom was the truth. I was being sincere.

"It's boring in prison."

"Seems like it would be."

I imagined her sitting in a cell. An old white woman missing teeth laying on her bed. Staring at the bunk above her. Waiting for time to pass. What a strange punishment, forcing a fellow human to lay in bed and wait for time to pass. Knowing when they got out a period of years had been stolen from their life. A person is living out their life in the world, their life doesn't turn out in a way that is conducive to behaving in a way that is permitted by the social contract established by its citizens whose lives turned out better. They commit a crime at a certain age. A court and its lawyers decide that they must leave society. That society would be better off without them. That must be a horrible feeling. Society notifying them that they are not wanted. Society does not want them so much they must be put in a cage in a large facility. They must be guarded by people carrying large cans of mace, sticks, and outside people with guns wait for them. Barb wire electric fences line the facility. They are pulled into the compound wearing hand cuffs chained up like an animal. Some humans decide that fellow humans are no good, so terrible they must be treated like animals.

The human made into animal sits inside her cell. She waits there like an animal. Fed like an animal, clothed like an animal, housed like an animal. They are so much like an animal they cannot even house themselves. They cannot control themselves like animals. The court decided that the woman across from me was at some point so horrible, she was not in control of herself to the point that she needed to be treated like an animal.

She didn't seem like an animal to me. She looked like a human, she had the form of a human. She talked, perhaps not perfect English, but it was common American English. Society had cast her out, had exiled her. That must have felt horrible to be treated like an animal.

She stopped talking after awhile and we both went to sleep.

Several hours late the bus stopped for us to eat. I woke up and went outside to smoke.

The convict was there smoking.

The sky was overcast. It was cold. We were wearing winter coats. Her coat was given to her by the prison. Her outfit wasn't worth five dollars.

I was lonely so I stood near her and talked.

"It's so nice to be walking around," she said

"What did you do to get in?"

"Writing bad checks."

"Four years for bad checks?" I said.

"The government don't like it when you write bad checks."

"Yeah, that's private property. Property is important to them."

"Well, I mean it's a long story. I wasn't always like that. I went to college for awhile when I was younger. I had kids. I was married."

"You were married?"

"Yeah, to a guy named John. John was a wonderful man. He worked at a warehouse and worked hard. He earned good money. We had a house and money to spend. We got along great. Even though we had kids it never drove us apart. I saw some of my friends get married and have kids, and it fucked up their marriages. Either the wife or the husband really didn't actually want kids. And they go away. But John was good. We both wanted our kids. We still had sex all the time. We still would sit up at night and talk about stuff. You know what I mean, like deeper stuff."

"Yeah, I've done that. It means a lot to talk to someone in the middle of the night about deeper stuff."

"Yeah, John was a good man. He would always know what to do. He could fix things. If the house needed shingles replaced, John wouldn't waste any time, he would go up there and fix those shingles. If something was broken on the car, John would be out there the next day to fix it. He was strong too. He would pick me up and flip me on his shoulder and carry me around like I was a sack of potatoes. And the whole time I would be laughing. You know, just giggling. John was a good man. He didn't make me work too much either. I always had a job working register 20 hours a week to get grocery money. But nothing serious. I enjoyed working. I liked seeing people besides the kids and John a little bit every week. But it was important for me to see John everyday. It was so important for me to get to touch him. I would do so many things for him. I would always make sure he had his favorite soda, Mountain Dew. The man had to have Mountain Dew. He loved mint chocolate chip ice cream. I always get that for him. He had to have chipped ham, never sliced, always chipped. See sweetie, I didn't have a great childhood. I can't really say my parents ever loved me. But John did, he loved me. He cared about me and I cared about him. But one day John came home and said he was dying of cancer. He was only 34. That was too young. We had been together for 12 years. Our oldest was 11. It didn't take long and he was dead."

"He died?"

"Yeah, like, he was gone. I watched him die. He was so sick in that hospital bed. They pumped him full of morphine, he couldn't feel it. But I could. I could feel his pain. I was scared. Then I was really scared when he left. I didn't know what to do. I started working 40 hours a week at a Wal-Mart and started doing drugs with the younger girls. I didn't know how to live without John," she started to cry. "I started doing drugs. And before you knew it I was writing fake checks to get money to buy drugs. When the police came for me I was coked out of my mind. They put me in a cage and I kept screaming for John. John never came though. He was dead."

We went inside the gas station/food court.

It was a large building with a high ceiling and bad lighting. I didn't want to eat there because I knew the food was going to be expensive but I was starving. I went and got some pizza and sat down. The convict came over and sat next to me and said, "That girl is getting that guy his food and paying for it."

"They never met before today," I said.

"No, they never met before," the convict said, giggling.

"The pizza was expensive."

"Yeah, I know. I ain't got much money."

"What you going to do now?"

"I don't know. You know I haven't had sex in four years."

"That's a long time."

"I know. I'm dying for it. I need to have sex. I love sex. John would have sex with me all the time. I don't feel right without sex."

"A lot of people don't."

"It never occurred to me how much I like sex until I was sitting in prison for a year, and I could just feel it down there rumbling, screaming for some dick."

"Screaming for dick?"

"Sweety, let me tell you. I would sit in that bottom bunk and just daydream for hours about dick. All I wanted was some dick. I didn't care about going to amusement parks or swimming in the ocean. I just wanted some dick, some love, some anything."

"Prison can be hard on a person's genitals."

"I don't know what it is. I mean, you get naked and someone fucks your pussy and it makes a fucking mess. The sheets are everywhere. Your hair gets all fucked up. You smell like sweat. You're all sticky down in your pants. But I missed it. I like to see naked men walking around my house. I like to see their hairy bodies and their penis wobble a little as they walk. I like when he's naked for me too, he's taken it all off and crawls all over me," she said.

"I like to touch women. Sometimes I get lonely and that's all wanna do. Is just touch a woman, all over."

"Oh sweety, you're telling me. I was so lonely in prison. So scared sometimes, so worried, so stressed out. Around that third year I was convinced I was gonna die in there. I don't know what got me through. I was so lonely and all I wanted to do was see a naked man come towards me and feel his dick slide up in me."

"That's reasonable."

"I really want to have sex," she said giving me a funny look.

I looked at her and thought she was crazy. She was trying to get me to have sex with her on a Greyhound bus as it passed through Pennsylvania. I was at least 15 years young than her. But I was bored and lonely and hadn't had sex in a long time and said, "I don't know if we can have sex, but I'll finger fuck you."

She said, "You serious?"

"Yeah, why not?"

She clapped her hands and said, "Hot damn."

Which was a bit dramatic.

We finished eating our expensive pizza and went back to the bus.

We sat next to each other. She had a funny shit-grinning look on her face. She was really happy. She had been in prison for four years and in less than a day she was breaking a law by finger fucking on a bus.

I slipped my hand in her pants.

She slipped her hand in my pants.

I touched my finger tips to her vagina.

It was shaved. I imagined her shaving her pussy in a prison shower with a cheap plastic razor.   I could see her telling some of her fellow inmates that when she got out she would get some dick and they would love her shaved pussy.

She cupped my penis, then rubbed it up and down.

Her vagina became wet. I slowly slipped my fingers in.

I had not had sex in so long that I had forgotten what a wet pussy felt like. There's something magical about a wet pussy. You can't help but think, "Her pussy is wet for me." It instills a sense of pride and one's self-esteem can't help but rise a little, at least for an hour.

My fingers were in her pussy swirling around in her wetness.

Her hand pumped my penis. I looked down at her hand in my pants and wanted to laugh. But I decided that was impolite and laughed inside my head.

She giggled and said, "Maybe you should get off the bus with me."

"I don't know. I have to meet friends there."

She looked sad and said, "You don't think we can fuck?"

"It doesn't seem like it's possible, it's still daylight outside."

She looked sad again, "Well, I'm happy you're finger fucking me."

"It is good."

Eventually I grew tired of finger fucking her and of her touching my penis. I just didn't care. She wasn't attractive and I didn't even know her name. She was a sad old woman and I was a sad young man. It made me depressed that we were both so sad we had to finger fuck and give handjobs on a Greyhound bus to feel okay about life.

I took my hand out of her pants and she took her hand out of mine.

We sat together for awhile.

Her head was on my shoulder and my hand was on her leg.

It was emotional but in a real pathetic way.

I went back to my seat and pretended to sleep. I wasn't good with women. I used to be a long time ago. I had confidence and a will to assert myself on others when I was in my early twenties. I would go to the bar and meet women. I would talk with women about things like music, books, and philosophy. We would get drunk and go home together. Sometimes I would date one of them. Then we would break up and I would have drunk sex with women again. But time passed and life beat me down. My brother killed himself, I never saw my parents again, I didn't have health care. I didn't have a good job. I didn't know what to do with my life. My life had no focus or clarity and wasn't very satisfying. I lost confidence in myself. Women like confidence. Women like men who have some focus in life, even poor women prefer men who want to get promoted at the beer can factory. I didn't even care about being promoted at a pizza shop. The world finds lazy people like me who want to write alone in rooms and cry to blues songs somehow an affront to the social contract, to the state of affairs of society.

The bus arrived on the border of Jersey. The woman and I both got off the bus to smoke. We didn't even say goodbye. We didn't even tell each other our names. She lit a cigarette and walked to another bus and I stood outside the bus smoking. She was gone. It was anonymous sex. Everyone on the bus was anonymous. The bus driver was paid to drive me across America and I didn't even know his name. I was in an anonymous town. And to everyone else I was anonymous. No one knew me standing there outside the bus on the border of Jersey.

I was going to be in New York soon. There were people there waiting for me. Tom White, the publisher of my first book, would be at the bus stop. Tom White was 50 years old. He was short with long hippy hair. I don't think he was a hippy. I think you had to be older for that and I don't recall him ever mentioning Janis Joplin or taking acid. He was from Bakersfield, California. He grew up in the desert. His father ran off when he was little to become a physicist. Hu Chin's father was a physicist also. I was surrounded by men with physicist fathers and my father was a meat cutter at K-mart. It was daunting knowing that they came from the penis of a physicist and I came from the penis of a meat cutter.

Tom was raised by his mother. She was a narcissistic high school teacher of English. She didn't spend quality time with little Tom. She would let him do what he wanted. Sometimes she would enter the room he was in and talk about things that did not concern Tom. Tom's mother eventually had several more kids with several more men that she did not concern herself with.

Tom White, his brother, sister and mother all lived in the same house barely communicating with each other. Tom would walk around the yard trying to find something to do but there was nothing to do. Sometimes he would sit in the summer on the brown baked grass and stare at his shoes.

He would walk down the street and look up the giant sky that hangs over Bakersfield and feel incredibly small. He knew there wasn't another real town for 500 miles. There wasn't anything but desert for ten hours of driving.

He would lay in his bed on hot summer nights when it was 110 degrees and cough on the dry air wishing he was dead he felt so suffocated by the endless nothing that was Bakersfield. He lived a loveless, alienated, heartbreaking life in the desert. His father had left. His mother was concerned with other things. A desert isn't like a forest, where a person can escape amongst the trees, creeks, and escape at the sight of a deer or an animal scurrying up a tree. It isn't like living on the edge of the ocean where a person can swim, see waves crashing in, and look at the sun rising or setting on an endless blue stage. It isn't like growing up in the Midwest amongst farms where one sees endless corn and beans being grown to provide sustenance for humanity. The Rust Belt even though it has its streets of rusted factories, cities full of empty houses, it is still wooded and a short drive by car can get you to the forest, large rivers and to The Great Lakes.

The desert offers nothing but a barren wasteland. To an outsider the desert might seem like a beautiful and wondrous thing to drive through. I drove through the American desert many times going out west and back. And each time I enjoyed gazing at the endless rocks, small mountains standing in the distance and the strange bushes at the rest stops. But it never occurred to me that it was a place to live. That my soul would flourish in such a place. And I especially did not ever think that growing up there would be awesome.

But Tom White grew up there. He grew up in the desert.

Tom escaped to Berkeley College and found friends and a life where he wasn't tortured by his mother or his peers. He enjoyed life at Berkeley but realized in his early 20s he wanted completely out of California. Most people believe that California is the apex of the American way of life. That to live in California is a dream come true and if they can just get to that sunny liberal place heaven will grant them happiness, security, and a meaning in life. Tom didn't find California to be that place.

Tom went to New York City. It was the early seventies and things were still happening. He moved into a small apartment on Saint Mark's. He hung out with writers, artists, and musicians. He worked in record and book shops. Bakersfield was gone. The big endless sky that his life took place under for so many years was replaced by the corridors of skyscrapers containing offices with storefront restaurants and clothing shops. He liked the congestion, the rampant pace, people everywhere, walking around in a hurry. He liked all the different races he could see and how they got along better than one race could in the small town of Bakersfield. He eventually got a job working in an office doing invoices and found a way to make money.

He had been living in a New York City a long time when I got off the bus underneath Times Square.

I got off the bus about 50 feet underground. Tom White was standing there leaning on a wall. I considered telling him about the 40 year old woman's pussy I finger fucked but decided it was too weird and dysfunctional and it didn't really make any sense.

I yelled, "Tom!"

He yelled back, "Benny Baradat."

We embraced each other. He was smaller than me and I felt his frail body in my arms. We shook hands softly, not with a firm grip. I always shook people's hands. Which surprised the people of New York City. It was always very important that people shook each other's hands in Youngstown. Perhaps because Youngstown was more violent than New York City and people in Youngstown might actually be carrying weapons.

Tom said, "How was your ride?"

"It was fine. I sat there and listened to the CD player. Sometimes the CD player worked, sometimes it didn't."

We walked out into Times Square. There it was, in all its glory. The lights, the big absurd advertisements, the restaurants, the tourist shops, The American Dream. Times Square was this huge church dedicated to capitalism, commercialism, corporatism, marketing, and absurdity. People would come from all over the world to gaze upon that church of commercialism called Times Square. Everything screamed "BUY SOMETHING." It was all seven deadly sins rolled into one place, lust, gluttony, vanity, sloth, greed, envy, and even wrath. A marketer trained in the dark arts during The Gilded Age decided to turn the square into Lucifer's very own playground. It's been said by people who actually grew up in New York City that Time Square is a porthole to hell. And that on Friday the 13th if you go to Times Square and say, "Bloody Mary" 20 times in a row a lesser demon will pop out and tell you to buy Paris Hilton perfume. And you will be forced to buy perfume and sometimes even an iPhone even if you already have one.

Tom White and I walked down the street, I said, "Where are the people? There's usually people everywhere. So many fucking people I usually can't stand it."

Tom said, "They disappeared, after October."

"Who, the tourists?"

"Yeah, it's only real New Yorkers now."

"Is this a real depression? I've never lived through a depression. I've received a terrorist attack, two wars and a tech and housing bubble pop but no depression."

"I'm 50 and never lived through a depression either. I got the Vietnam War and several more oil price spikes than you," Tom said.

"I don't think this will be good."

"They are bleeding money so they are only having us work three days a week. I thought about looking for another job but they've laid off 100,000 stock brokers and hedge funders who can do invoices a thousand times better than me."

We walked away from Times Square to the lower east side. The scenery changed from an overload of advertisements to a normal New York City amount.

Tom said, "How is college going?"

"Good, I like getting up early, going to campus, buying coffee and a muffin and walking to class. I like walking around the campus. I like looking at the young girls. The young girls don't look at me. But I look at them like a creepy old man."

"The young girls are always nice."

After saying that I realized New York City is like a giant college campus. Everyone walking around from destination to destination, young girls walking around everywhere. Everyone stopping to get coffee and eat pastries. I didn't say it out loud though.

"I remember thinking college was going to be really hard. Everyone would talk about how hard it was going to be. It wasn't. It was high school plus a couple more pages of work, " said Tom White.

"No, it isn't hard. Showing up is the hardest thing. That's what life is about though, showing up, being on time, doing what needs to be done."

"People have been trying to make life more than that since the beginning of humanity. We try to pretend that when we make a peanut butter sandwich somehow God is watching and giving it meaning. But it really requires that we go to work, make money. Buy the bread and peanut butter. And walk from where we were sitting in our house to the kitchen and making the sandwich. Nothing really happens."

"Nothing ever happens. Maybe this depression will change that," I said.

"It probably won't."

"Maybe there will be civil unrest."

"Look around Benny," Tom pointed to the people walking by and said, "Everyone is walking around consumed with their own personal interest. The Americans that are alive have known nothing but their own personal interest. The only thing that ties us together is The Constitution. Which means what? We point at that document and say, 'We believe in a democratic republic, we believe in the separation of powers, the separation of church and state, we believe we have certain inalienable rights that cannot be taken away.' Let's look at what that means, a democratic republic means we believe in voting in a few who can afford to take a year off of their lives just to campaign to represent the many, so we believe in an oligarchy. We believe in separating power so we don't have to constantly fight each other, and we believe in rights and not in doing things. I don't think that is bad. The system has worked for me. America doesn't have a lot of internal conflict. The system is stable, the roads are paved and the police have never brought me in for treason. But there isn't anything that binds us. We have no universal *raison d'etre* here. We have a voice and we have rights and we even have protection. But nothing gives us meaning. An Arab in Iraq or a Catholic in Peru walks to the kitchen to make a sandwich God watches them. God says, 'Thou shall eat a sandwich because I've made you hungry.' When a Chinese person walks to the kitchen to make a sandwich they are staying alive, remaining strong, to honor the ancestors, for the beauty and legacy that is China. When an American walks to the kitchen to make a sandwich, what do they tell themselves, they are doing it for the free exercise of religion. For the ability to not have to testify against oneself, to bear arms. No, an American walks to the kitchen and makes a sandwich and that's all. There is no reason to it. It is absolutely meaningless. When an Arab in Iraq or a Catholic in Peru go to the market to buy food, they see their fellow Muslims and Catholics, those who love, pray, and have devoted themselves to the same function as them, to serve their God. When a Chinese person goes to the market they see their fellow communists, their fellow Chinese who have kept China running for three thousand years. What do we see at the market? Other people who believe in free-market capitalism? We have no roots. We have no real history. A Brazilian can at least say they are part of the history of

Catholicism. An institution that has lasted for 200 years and shows no sign of disappearing. The Arabs have history, theirs goes back all the way to the ancients. To Persia, to ancient Egypt. We might feel horrified by the Indian religion and their caste system, but their religion and caste system has sustained them for three thousand years. There is something about an ancient institution that gives a person a place in history. And knowing you are in history makes you recognize that people came before you and people will come after you. That the lakes, oceans, mountains, and the soil were before you, and if you don't destroy them they will be there after you. There is no sense of time in The Constitution. The Christian Bible is nothing but time, it starts at the birth of the universe, traces generation after generation of good and bad behavior, of foolishness, of folly, of heroism, of greatness. And it ends with the end of time. The history of the Catholic church, of Islam, of Buddhism, the histories of European nations and China. Those people are reared in history. It never occurs to people that maybe all these other countries are poorer than America, because they see no point in being rich as America. Knowing that you are part of history, also lets you know that being rich and being consumed with your own self-interest does not really matter. It is good to have security, comfort, a place to live, and some food to eat. But it doesn't really matter. Before you were born everyone got along without you, and when you die, and are nothing but bones, everyone will get along without you. You aren't that important. You might be important if you did something or treated people in a way that left your mark on further generations. But owning an expensive apartment or the newest coolest cell phone will not cause that. The Constitution does not teach us that. The Constitution does not teach us about time. The Constitution does not mention time, it doesn't even mention history, it is meant to be a timeless document that can be applied to any situation in history, but does not create a way we can view our own lives and the lives of others with any sense of meaning. It is nothing but procedures and the granting of rights. Americans don't have a sense that we are in history together, and more than just those who are alive, but those who have come before and those who will come after. There is no poetry in The Constitution. Religion has poetry, the story of Job, the stories of Hindu gods, the stories of the Buddha and the Buddhists who came after, and the Koran. Those books may not make sense to our empirical American minds. But they contain laws, that other people dead and living have assumed to be worth living by. Just like we assume The Constitution is worth living by. But there is no poetry in The Constitution. A person can lose everything, they can be on the street homeless crying, their wife gone, their kids, their job gone, and they can think of the story Job, they can cry, and find hope. And they can tell themselves that life is still worth living. But you can't be homeless, wife gone, kids gone, and job and think of the Second Amendment, start crying and find hope. Americans think that with the application of enough sociological, psychological, and biological theories and remedies mankind will just feel great about being alive. A political philosophy may design the perfect procedure so that everyone is treated equally. But that's not what humanity really wants, learning the Labeling Theory in a classroom or on television is not the same as when David was labeled a little man, a teenager, worth nothing, but he didn't allow the label of being young and small to deter his will to take on life, to take charge of his destiny and kill Goliath. A person can read that and cry. A person can find hope and courage in that story. I have no problem and fully support research and the creation of theories to better humanity. But everyone, even those who make those theories want something more out of life," Tom said.

"There's a schizophrenic in Youngstown, an old black man, that walks around saying he's The U.S. Constitution. They used to say they were God or Jesus," I said.

"There is no meaning to our lives. We have procedures to keep us safe from ourselves, we have rights, but we don't have meaning. We fill this lack of meaning with objects. We survey the landscape and find nothing but objects, gadgets to fill our sense of nihilism. Our constitution doesn't supply that emotional element that binds humans to each other. Ask a Mexican what he is, what his best friend, what his brother is, he points at a church. The Chinese point at an ancient temple, the European at an ancient church or something the Romans built. Something that binds them together as a people that live temporarily on earth."

Tom stopped in front of a restaurant and we went in. It was an Italian restaurant that didn't serve any of the known Italian foods in Youngstown. None of the servers were Italian or even New Yorkers. All of them had foreign accents. I believe our waiter was French. I ordered a diet Pepsi and Tom ordered water. I decided on the spinach pesto raviolis and Tom got some weird vegan thing.

I said, "But do you believe this leads to nihilism?"

"The Constitution is without emotion. It gives humanity procedures that reduce the possibility of violent conflict. It allows for the freedom of man and gives him a reason to flourish. But it doesn't give us beauty, it doesn't have poetry, it doesn't create an emotional bond between us. And that is what nihilism is, it is life without emotion. The Declaration of Independence says we get these rights from God. But it doesn't tell the story of a man wandering in the wilderness for forty years, going through great travails, suffering to bring us this message. This message from God comes from really rich white men who owned slaves, and had so much money they could sit for months doing nothing but talking. Because that is what the story is, there's the war and everything. But the constitution is not the story of men going through hell, sitting alone in the desert speaking to the gods, fasting and living with inner turmoil like the prophets. No, it's the story of very rich white men sitting around talking and bitching at each other. Compare it to the story of the French Revolution, the peasants coming together after years of oppression to fight the nobles. The Storming of the Bastille. The immense struggle that took place to recreate their country into one that people could live in. It is a powerful story that the oppressed can hang onto, they can cry over, that they can share a drink over. That perhaps all the oppressed of the world can share a drink over. But where is the emotion in The Constitution? There is none."

"But we drink at the Fourth of July. We have fireworks, we have parties, and barbecue."

"So is that our religion, the government?"

"Well, we still have the Protestants. They're going strong," I said.

"That isn't an ancient religion though. That's Elmer Gantry crap. There is no history in American Protestantism. Their Jesus isn't an ancient Jew that lives in the desert and shits in an outhouse. That religion was created on this land 120 years ago. Their Jesus isn't a homeless Jesus. Their Jesus is this hard working man who has short hair and combs it to the left. He wears suits. He gets up everyday and works. He plays the game. Their Jesus believes that working for owners, doing what they're told without question to get raises to buy more crap is the apex of the religious experience. They believe Jesus has actually blessed them when they get granted a loan for a Hummer. They believe in a Loan God. The God that grants loans, that supplies credit, that supplies air-conditioning and allows a person to turn their heat up to 72. It isn't a God of suffering. The poetics are there, the emotion is there, they are bound by their belief in their capitalist God. But history isn't there. No one enters a Protestant church and thinks, 'This is an old religion created by a Jew 2,000 years ago.' You enter a Catholic church and can't help thinking that you've entered a very old tradition. When the priest comes out wearing those funny clothes, one can see this establishment goes back a very long time."

"But Catholics are very much about procedure."

"But is it procedure or ritual? What's the difference. That's the question. A procedure is this lifeless thing that humans must go through so it liquidates human emotion so that we don't kill each other. Rituals are these things humans do that create emotional bonds between fellow humans so that they don't kill each other."

"But the Eucharist is nonsense. The blood and body of Christ turned into a wafer. There's no sense to that, we want to make sense now."

"But do humans want to make sense? We have lived on this planet for 100,000 years not making any fucking sense, then 350 years ago, like 10 white guys wrote some things down that made sense. And our Founding Fathers decided to write up a document that made sense. Then some other European nations decided to make sense, then they went all over the earth forcing everyone at gun point to make sense without ever asking them if they wanted to make sense."

"Are you saying we don't want to make sense?"

"They like science. They like the science of air-conditioners, of cars, of plastic baggies, of cell phones, they like the science that goes into making products. They like the procedures that reduce violence amongst humans. But they don't like viewing the world in such a way that when they make a peanut butter sandwich alone in their kitchen, it means nothing. That when their child dies, or they foreclose on their house, or when their car gets repossessed, or when life turns into shit that it means nothing. A Muslim having a bad day can walk next door and pray with his fellow Muslim. Then they tell stories to each other of past Muslims and their trials through life. An American stands in his kitchen and holds his toaster he bought with a credit card asking the object to give him his prestige back."

"But these procedures have created a safe world."

"No, I'm not saying that at all. There are many countries that have a lot of governmental procedures that created safety, and limit conflict to heated debate and not guns. But Europe, South America and Asia supply their citizens with a sense of history. Our nation doesn't supply that. There is no cross-cultural emotional link between the office worker in New York City, the factory worker in Ohio, the farmer in Nebraska and the camera man in California. When something bad happens there is nothing that binds us together."

"But that is everywhere, that is the reason for nationalism."

"So God has died, and with it, all His beautiful literature of courage and hope. And instead of rebuilding literature to show us how to create our lives, we focus on creating the perfect procedures."

Our food came and we chewed and swallowed. We stopped talking about government and talked of movies we had seen recently. He discussed Fassbinder, Goddard, and other long forgotten film makers that no one cares about anymore. He sent me some burned DVDs in the mail, I watched them and told him my impressions. I confessed that all I really watch are movies starring small Asians kicking people's asses.

We finished our food and walked out onto the street. It was around 12 and I needed to meet Petra. She was a woman I met through writing. She was a friend of a guy in Austin, Texas who published some of my writing two years before. She read the writing and emailed me. She wrote long emails about feelings and what she did during the day. Petra's emails were always wrought with emotion and sensitivity. Most of the time when people emailed me, they either told me they liked my writing or asked me to read something they wrote. I rarely ever read what people wrote. I would skim it to see if I liked it, but no matter what I wrote back that I liked it. I saw no reason to be mean to someone. Most people never decide to express themselves through writing, why deter people from doing it.

I liked Petra's emails. They were soothing. She showed me pictures of herself on Photobucket. She was an attractive half-Korean half-white women. She had black hair, pretty lips, small Asian eyes, and a small Asian body. She also had an amazing butt.

We wrote emails to each other off and on. Sometimes we wouldn't write for months, but then we would write again.

She had a strange story: Her father was a soldier in the Navy. He was stationed in South Korea guarding the South Koreans from the North Koreans. He met Petra's mother at a bodega. A little stand selling coffee to soldiers. The two began having sex with each other even though they couldn't speak each other's language. Petra said her mother wanted to get to America no matter what. Her mother was obsessed with money and wanted to have security and wealth. So she intentionally chose to work at the bodega selling coffee to soldiers so she would meet one and get married.

Petra's parents started having sex and spending a lot of time with each other. Petra's mother eventually became pregnant with Petra. Petra's parents got married in South Korea and she was born. Her parents didn't care about her. Her mother viewed her as a way to get to America. Petra walked around South Korea in the slums talking to old men and throwing rocks through the windows of abandoned buildings. She spoke Korean and only heard English when her father would talk to her, which was rarely.

When Petra was three she came to America. Her father was from Tennessee, so that's where they went. Not to one of the fun states like California, Florida, or New York but to a godforsaken state like Tennessee.

When Petra and her parents arrived in America her father moved on. He hung around until she was eight but left because he didn't care. Petra didn't watch him leave. She came home from school and he wasn't there. Her mother cried and Petra cried. Little Petra was heartbroken. The first man that she loved and supposedly loved her, was gone.

Petra's mother brought her sister over to America and they opened a gas station together. Her mother opened and bought gas stations all over the Tennessee area. Her mother was a determined capitalist. She wanted money and figured out how to get it. Her mother understood that money came from owning businesses. That one needed to accumulate businesses and to pay the workers cheaply and offer good services. Her mother would work 12 to 14 hours a day to keep her businesses running. She wanted security and to own nice things. Her mother married an overweight lawyer when Petra was 12 . The lawyer would sit and smoke cigarettes and not care about anything while watching television after work. He was polite to Petra though and showed her courtesy. He wasn't the type of man that sat with her and showed her how to play sports or brought her to museums. But he wasn't mean. When Petra was 17 he died of a heart attack. The second man that showed up, showed her love and she showed love to was gone. She was heartbroken again.

The summer before she went to New York City for a small vacation and fell in love with the place. She knew she had found a new place to live with new adventures. She saved up some money and found an apartment with a friend from Austin who had just moved there.

At that time she was running through her savings and still hadn't found a job. She was living on the lower-east side with a girl named Lyndi Wood. Lyndi Wood was a woman who grew up in Oregon. Her father was a big time lawyer and made a lot of money. He made so much money he sent Lyndi Wood to Stanford and Lyndi didn't have to take out any college loans. Her father was paying for her to live in New York City. He would put money in an account every week. The bill for the apartment was sent to him and not to her. She was supposed to be looking for a job as a journalist. She wasn't doing anything but drinking.

11.

I buzzed the door and waited. Tom was looking down the street at a sign. Tom was wishing he was buzzing the door of a woman in her 30s. But we both knew that one day I would be 50 and not buzzing any young women's doors anymore.

The door opened and I said, "Tom, I'll see you in two days."

He came over and hugged me and said, "See ya, in two days."

I walked into the apartment building. There were stairs leading up. I looked up to see if she came out. She was standing on the third floor wearing no shoes. Looking down at me with a small smile. I smiled back trying to be as pleasant as possible and walked up.

We stood within three feet of each other and Petra said, "I wish my vagina was a cappuccino machine."

I replied, "I wish someone would pay my car insurance for me."

We went in her apartment. It was small. It had a kitchen and two bedrooms. There was no television just a radio hooked to an iPOD. There was no kitchen table. Some magazines and a book shelf, that was all.

Her roommate Lyndy came out. She had brown hair and pale skin. Her eyes were large and didn't look at anything particular. Lyndy said, "Petra says you're here to get your picture taken for a magazine."

I said, "True."

"Well, that is great. That is really exciting. Are you excited?"

I considered if I was excited or not and said, "I feel pretty good about it. It is better than not getting your picture taken for a magazine."

"That's great. Well, I got stuff to do, I'll go back to my room."

Lyndy went back to her small room.

Petra took me to her small room. Nothing could fit in the room but a bed and a computer. There was nothing but a cheap clock on the wall. It was very stark and cell like.

Petra sat down at the computer and checked things on the Internet. She said without looking at me, "You know *The Republic* right?"

"The one by Plato or Cicero?"

"The one by Plato."

"Yeah, who doesn't?"

"You know that line, 'finding it hard to die' in book three?"

"That's a good line."

"The other day I had an interview with an employer. It was some silly thing, to work helping the mentally disabled for like 13 dollars an hour. I was sitting there and the boss guy kept talking. And asking me these really nonsensical questions. Describing all these procedures and I all I could think was, 'finding it hard to die.' I couldn't focus. I kept stumbling through my answers."

"Did you have a nice outfit on, that's what really matters in those situations."

"My hair and make-up looked very good. I didn't look slutty and I didn't look proletariat. I looked like a woman who could work."

"Did you get hired?"

"I haven't heard back from them yet. I walked home from the place. It was uptown. I just kept walking, talking to myself, saying, 'finding it hard to die' over and over again. Like if I said it enough it would extinguish me. It's December though: and no birds were singing. There wasn't any snow. There wasn't any rain. The sky was gray and had no point. People walked by. I looked at them. Many of them had jobs. I assume they had jobs or they wouldn't be living in New York. I had no job and they had jobs. That was the score. And since I was 'finding it hard to die' I had to get a job."

I looked down at my shoes and said, "Maybe you will get a job soon."

"I don't know if there are jobs. I'm not even sure what a job is. I came to this city to be a New Yorker. I wanted to drink and walk around looking cute. What a thing to want, to drink and look cute. To feel intoxicated and to have men look at me and think, 'boy she is cute.' While I am thinking, 'finding it hard to die.' Which leads to me drinking more than I should. It makes me feel better though."

"The men thinking you're cute."

"Yes, the men. I like when other people that are not me, think good thoughts about me. I have tried all my life to break that habit. But it so nice to be sitting there at a bar with a man telling you sweet things. I like to hear sweet things about myself. I like to be flattered. I like when men buy me drinks and dinner. It shows me that they are going to work at some stupid job not only to pay their bills, but they consider it important that they show up and perform meaningless tasks for the sake of buying me drinks and dinner."

"Don't expect me to buy you drinks and dinner. I don't have the money."

"I know you won't. You don't care if I'm pretty. Usually men come in here and start saying all kinds of crazy shit about me being attractive and wonderful and smart. You just came in and sat down not giving a shit about flattering me at all. I'm not used to it. But it is fun to have a new experience every once and awhile."

While not looking at her I said, "I do consider you attractive. But I assume you've been told that before. And probably already know you're attractive."

"You like to not tell me I'm attractive. You know that people tell me that and it makes me feel good. And you deprive me of that flattery because you know it disorients me and pisses me off. You're enjoying pissing me off."

"I have screwed cute, ugly, fat and skinny girls. And it is my experience that whether or not the experience was worth it was not based on how the girl looked. I once screwed a hairy girl and had a lot of fun. If you want to screw someone or love someone just because they are attractive, then why not masturbate to porn where all the women are attractive and you don't have to buy them drinks and dinner?"

"Do you want to masturbate on me?"

"Do you want to tell yourself that I ejaculated because you are so attractive?"

"I like to be thought of as attractive and I prefer when men have huge orgasms on or in me," said Petra.

"But you're taking advantage of your endowments then. You are endowed with a beautiful face and body because of no doing of your own. It is not your fault you're attractive. Being happy about that is like a rich kid being happy because they have a huge apartment and expensive education because their parents paid for it. It is capitalistic. You view your own body as capital."

"My body is capital."

"I'm fucking with you because I'm not that attractive. I've never been known as attractive. People don't talk about Benny being attractive."

"You're okay looking."

"When I smile my face makes all these weird lines."

"Don't smile."

"I try not to, but when people take pictures you're supposed to smile, so I smile, and my face looks bad and then they post it on the Internet," I said.

"That is bad."

"I know. I saw that Youtube video you made, you were walking around with a chicken in Texas."

"I like chickens."

"When I was little my family had chickens. It wasn't like a chicken farm. There was only like five hens and two roosters. My dad would make me feed them and bring them water."

"When I lived in Tennessee my neighbors had chickens. They would walk into our yard. Chickens are like cats they seem to be concerned with their own things."

Petra went to the bathroom and put make-up on. I sat and looked around her room. It didn't seem like a big deal that I was with her. She didn't seem like an asshole. There seemed no chance of marrying her and impregnating her. It was life. She was there and I needed the friendship of a woman.

12.

      We slowly walked down the sidewalk with meaningless steps. It was different than walking with Tom White. With Tom it was serious. The city was a disaster. New York was a nightmare of futility and gluttony. Walking beside Petra it was a different city. New York had become a romantic city full of meaning and purpose. It became a city where people could fall in love. She was not the kind of person that cared about the philosophical constructs of the United States Constitution. She didn't watch cable news programs analyzing the daily events. Petra didn't read Hegel or Wittgenstein. I didn't have to engage in intellectual conversation that would force me to feel uncomfortable and talk out my ass at times. She wasn't uneducated though: she had a psychology degree and knew her profession well. She knew all the big words intellectuals say. I didn't have to watch how I spoke like I did when I was work. I didn't have to make sure I didn't appear a snob. She had her profession of psychology, case studies, cognitive behavior therapy, behaviorism, and abnormal psyche. I had my literature and political philosophy. So we met somewhere else, as two people that had a sincere love for life. It wasn't that we were both sophisticated, or knew about things or both had ambition. It was that life interested us.

      Snow started falling and I said, "New York is pretty with the snow falling."

      She responded, "It should be for how much I pay in rent to live here."

      Petra's eyes stared out of her head drifting and floating around. It was like she couldn't focus her gaze. They were eyes that wandered around the landscape looking for meaning. They weren't the strong eyes of a person that had authority and power. They weren't the cold intellectual eyes of an old dean of a philosophy department. And they weren't the eyes of an angry blue collar worker who never had authority and has worked with his hands all his life. They were a different kind of eyes. A lot of people in New York had them. They weren't the eyes of a person who could take control and make people do what they wanted. They were sad whimsical confused eyes, constantly scouring the landscape for more entertainment.

She had a small Asian body. It was thin and taut with muscle. It was so different than what I was used to. My experiences with the female body consisted of Northern European white girls who were wide and always had a little meat on them. And black girls with loads of muscle. The women I had dated could pick this woman up and smash her. I felt weird walking along with Petra's Asian body. Like I was betraying the strong bodies and hard eyes of the women back in Youngstown. I imagined them saying, "Look at Benny, what does he think he's doing walking around with that frail little bitch?"

We stopped in front a bar and Petra said, "Here it is, isn't it great?"

I looked at the bar and said, "It's small."

"All the bars are small here."

I threw my cigarette down and we went in.

We went up to the bar. The bartender had a mustache. Petra said, "You look like Freddie Mercury."

The guy was very excited and said, "You think so?"

"Oh, you look really good. Freddie Mercury was awesome."

He looked really happy. Several of the men had mustaches in the bar.

We got Pabst and sat on a couch.

I said, "Why does everyone have a mustache. Cops have mustaches. Have hipsters become obsessed with cops?"

"No, that's the new hipster apparel."

"We have beards in Youngstown."

"Beards are so two years ago."

"I like beards. I think men look good with beards," I said honestly.

"No, beards are gone."

"I don't like men with shaved faces, they look like penises."

"Yeah, they do. They look like flaccid penises."

"Like a sad weak penis that can't find a pussy."

"I don't think they are trying to look attractive with their mustaches."

"They are hip," I said.

"The mustache says, 'Look, I'm really trying to look stupid to look cool. Imagine how good I am in bed.'"

"When they give head you can feel hair brushing against the area above your vagina."

She looks off into the horizon and says, "I don't think I like that. When

89

it's short, it's all prickly. But if he has a bushy beard, you can't feel it."

"His mustache is prickly."

"Yeah, it is." She patted my knee and said, "Come on, lets go play video games."

It was the first time she had really touched me. I felt nervous. There was a woman and she was being nice to me. Every time I ever got into a situation like that. A situation where there is a woman and she is showing signs of possible sex mixed with alcohol I feel like a block of stone walking around all stone-like staring out of my head wondering what the hell I should be doing. I felt like running out of the building down the street calling Tom White on the phone and having him come to get me. Tom would never make me feel nervous. I would go in his apartment and he would give me a glass of water, a pillow and blanket and place to sleep.

Trying to be romantic with a real live human woman is a lot harder than reading Wittgenstein or doing political statistics. If you can't understand a concept in Wittgenstein you can Google it or go the library. Political statistics consist of math and constants. There are answers without contingencies with an empirical basis. Dealing with people is a lot harder. You never fucking know what they are going to do. They're out there not being you. They are just like you though, they are configuring, applying logic, acting, contriving, and they are capable of lying or switching their mind. I kept getting the urge to kiss her though. She knew I was a weak person without confidence and she was going to have to do everything. It seemed like a game to her.

We got more drinks and took shots. Everything became easier.

We sat next to each other on the couch again. We sat close, like we were lovers, like we had known each other for years and we were going to make love. I kept looking at her face and feeling happy. I would look at her eyes and she would look at my eyes and somehow that meant sex. I could never figure out why eyes meant sex, but they do.

A guy came over and started talking about a zombie movie. He asked Petra to be in it. Petra said she had been in a zombie movie once. I said I had been in a killer space alien movie once. The guy said he loved zombies. Petra also said she loved zombies. I clapped and said I loved zombies. Everyone was bonding over zombies. The guy kept talking to Petra about the movie. I didn't have anyone to talk to. I looked around the room and there were people playing pool. They looked like people but hipper versions. I wondered if they liked Dave Eggers. I imagined Dave Eggers and Jonathan Safran Foer coming in the bar and ordering Captain and Cokes. Foer looked beat down because of the long term failure of his last book.

Dave Eggers said, "But it sold a lot, you should be happy."

Foer responded, "But it only sold for like a year and half the reviewers said it was nonsense."

Eggers responds, "What the fuck does that matter?"

Foer says looking sadly at his beer, "But I don't want to be known as that guy who wrote two really topical books because his agent suggested writing on those topics."

Eggers responds without caring, "Seriously Jon you're like a pretty rich kid with connections and a good editor. How many pretty rich kid writers can you name who wrote books that transcended time?"

Foer rubbed his head, fixed his glasses and said, "Dostoevsky and Proust."

"They were ugly. Try again."

"Hmm, Albert Camus?"

"He was poor."

"You have the same problem as I do."

Dave Eggers responds politely, "No, I know my fate. I'm pretty and rich. I like to write. The world lets me write. I get lots of money and I can get laid easily. I'm not trying to be a great writer, I'm trying to live a great life."

Some guy came over to me with tattoos and a bowler hat and said, "I hear you like zombies and you write. You think you can write me a zombie movie?"

"Zombies," I said in monotone voice.

"Yeah, man, zombies. Like people are in a building and they are trapped with zombies."

"How about a movie about 30 normal people trapped in a high school with machines and a million dollars."

"Then what?"

"Then everyone kills each other for the money."

"That would be dumb."

"How about this, we call the movie *State of Nature*. The movie has a godlike creature who has a deal for humanity. The godlike creature has a resource that will allow everyone to drive and transport goods and grow more food than they ever dreamed of. But there's a catch after three generations the resource will run out and their entire civilization will collapse. Now it won't matter to them because they will be dead. But their great great grandchildren will die of starvation and violence because the resource will run out and all their motorized vehicles will stop running."

"I don't think anyone would make that deal."

"You don't think so?"

"No, of course not."

"What about a movie about a zombie that can't find anybody to eat. Like he keeps running around and when he sees somebody, everyone else gets there first. And he is like standing by a gas station pump looking depressed. Then all the other zombies come over and make fun of him."

"I wanna make the movie for like 2 million dollars," he said.

"I really like movies with a lot of CGI. I like CGI giant snakes tearing down trees and killing massive amounts of civilians."

"Oh, those are good," he said.

"You should make a movie about The DOW. Like The DOW becomes a monster that grows to an immeasurable size and eats everyone's souls through the use of well-orchestrated marketing and mob mentality. Then The DOW gets killed because his favorite food is going into depletion."

"Dude, that sounds great. We could probably get a big name actor for that."

"Oh yeah, totally. Probably get like Michael Cera. Michael Cera loves to do movies like that."

Petra came back over and said, "That guy said I could be in a zombie movie. I will have so many fan boys jerking off to my ass."

13.

Petra and I entered her apartment somewhat drunk. I didn't know what would happen. She had touched my knees and shoulders with her hands many times. I've hung out with women before who did the same thing and it ended in nothingness and despair.

We went in her bedroom. I sat on the bed with my feet on the wood floor. I took off my boots. She had never mentioned me sleeping on the small futon in the kitchen. She took off her shoes by the closet and sat down on the bed next to me.

I said, "Are we supposed to kiss now?"

She replied laughing, "I think so."

"I know I want to kiss you, like I've been thinking about it, imagining it. But I'm not you, so I don't know if you want to kiss me."

"I do want to kiss you," she said looking at me in the face.

"I suppose we have to kiss each other then, like we have to move our faces very close together, so close they touch. Then we open our mouths and stick out our tongues."

"Kissing is like a deal."

"Kissing and fucking are very much like a deal or contract."

We moved our faces close together. Our faces were close, they were inches apart. Her face touched mine, our lips touched and we kissed. Every time I kiss someone for the first time I compare them to everyone I've ever kissed. It goes back to my first kiss with Sarah Hill when I was 13 in her dinning room. She was dressed in her band uniform holding her flute case in her left hand. That was my favorite kiss. Then it moves onto the woman I almost married and how she kissed roughly with mental illness. Then I remember bad kisses with girls who barely stuck their tongues out and women who bit my tongue and made me hate them for doing that.

Petra wasn't a bad kisser. When beginning to kiss someone I always get nervous about what to touch with my hands. Should I touch her butt, tits, or arms? I chose to touch her butt with one hand and her back with the other. She seemed to enjoy that. She touched my back and ribs. I enjoyed that. It wasn't mad kissing like in the movies. We weren't estranged lovers that had found each other after years of tribulations. We were just two people trying to have a good time. Sex is about having a good time. A lot of people think sex is about being intimate. Sex is funny. Sex is smelly, loud, and funny. Intimacy is when you sit in the middle of the night with your lover and talk about embarrassing moments from your childhood you never say out loud. Or when you sit with your lover or friend who's sick for hours without ever thinking "this sucks" but being worried the whole time that your lover will be okay.

I took Petra's shirt off. It was a pretty sight. Her flesh was nice and dark. It wasn't tan, she was naturally dark. She smiled when I pulled her shirt off. Then I noticed a birthmark on her shoulder. She saw me looking at it and said, "Don't look at it. It's a birthmark."

"I seriously don't care if you have a birthmark."

"Are you sure?"

"No, I'm making it up."

"What if you can't have sex with me," said Petra.

"I don't think that will be a problem."

"It could be a problem," she said with concern.

"Do you repeat this dialogue every time you have sex with someone for the first time?"

"Yeah, so?"

"Well, after you've had this dialogue did the man not have sex with you?"

"Well, you might be different."

"Why would I be different?" I said.

"Because, I don't know."

"I don't care if you have a birthmark, I wouldn't care if you only had one arm."

"Are you serious?"

"No, I'm lying. I'm going to leave right now and get a hotel and a prostitute without a birthmark."

She laughed and said, "You're weird."

"I'm going to take your pants off now and it is going to be awesome."

"That sounds good."

I took her pants off. She lay there in her underwear and bra. I was hoping she would take her bra off herself because I hate doing that. I feel like I'm her slave taking her clothes off. Women never take my clothes off. Probably because I'm an ass. I stood up next to the bed and took my clothes off. I was standing there in my boxers. For some reason unknown to me and all of Western Civilization we feel it is important to do kissing and grinding in our undergarments before we fully take off our underwear. We kissed and rubbed our clothed genitals against each other but eventually we took off our underwear. It was predictable. Sex seemed so much like a math problem, it was disheartening at times. When having sex I came to wish something really weird would happen. Like she would start punching me in the face and tell me I was bad at cooking. Or get a coat hanger and beat me with it. Or run around the room throwing things at my head like lamps and computer monitors. Nothing like that ever happened.

After we took off all of our clothes she laid back and allowed me to put my penis in her wet vagina. It went easily. Every time my penis enters into a vagina I think, "This is serious, take this seriously, this is really happening, you are really having sex, Benny with another person that is not you or your hand or the girls on the Internet. You must focus and try to give the impression that you aren't nuts and can have sex like a normal person." I don't really like to have sex with my penis. It is an okay penis but not a real big one like a porn cock. Porn cocks are big and manly and awesome in their power. My penis holds no power. Her vagina was slightly tight, not like a girl in high school but it had maintained tightness over the years.

She said as she laid on her back, "Asian girls have tight pussies don't they? We never get loose."

"Do you have statistical evidence for that. Have you ran that through an SPSS or something?"

She laughed and thought I was being funny. I was being totally serious.

I started pumping her. I liked looking down at her pretty face. I kept touching her face while pumping. Touching her face didn't make me hot, I just liked touching it. She made noises. I enjoyed hearing her noises. I tried to tell myself that those noises came from my sweet cock, but I knew getting a girl to make noises during sex wasn't that hard.

Then I laid on my back and she got on top. She pumped really hard. She was in a lot better shape than I was. I was panting and dying for a cigarette. I felt fat and that I needed to run laps. She kept pumping, going crazy, her butt wiggling, her belly flexing. I really liked her being on top because if it was bad sex then it was her fault.

Eventually I ate her vagina. I liked my head in between her thighs. Her thighs were little and strong. They were different than the big boned thighs of white and black women. I couldn't recall if I ever had sex with such a little woman. The woman I was going to marry was short, only 5 feet tall. But she was mostly Northern European and a quarter estranged Israeli Jew and had some meat on her. Petra was definitely the smallest woman in bone structure that I had ever sex with. It was a new experience. A foreign one. She had sex just like white and black women but her body felt different when it touched mine. It was a strange experience causing just as many thoughts as arousal.

Petra went down on me. I always get scared the girl will bite my penis, instead of having a really great time I feel nervous. I looked down at her cute Asian head sucking my penis and felt a sense of pride. It was irrational and reasonless but I felt it anyway.

She stopped and her face came up to mine and we kissed. I really loved kissing her. I really liked the present, there was nothing terrible about laying there naked with her, half drunk, giving each other head and kissing.

We pulled the blankets over us. I spooned Petra.

14.

It was morning, I was laying in bed with my clothes on when Petra got back from the store with eggs and vegetables. She made coffee and poured orange juice. I sat on the futon in the kitchen and listened to her talk about money. I sat and drank coffee. She stood over the stove cooking eggs mixed with green peppers, mushrooms and cheese.

Then the smoke alarm started going off. Petra got up on a stool and played with it. Her playing with it did nothing to help the problem. Lyndi Wood kept yelling from her bedroom to take the battery out. Petra said to me, "Benny, get up here and do this. I need to take care of the eggs."

I got up on the stool. I stood on the stool playing with the smoke alarm. Most of it was made of plastic with little red wires and something that looked like a battery. The battery would not come out so I ripped it out. The alarm didn't stop. I said to Petra while looking at the alarm, "What the fuck is wrong with this thing? I took the fucking battery out."

She looked up at the alarm and said, "Punch it."

"It's made of plastic, my hand will get all cut up."

"Hmm, rip the whole thing out of the ceiling."

I attempted to rip the whole thing out of the ceiling but nothing happened. The alarm persisted without remorse to make terrible electronic noises. I said, "That's all I can do. Just finish cooking quickly."

"I don't like to rush cooking. I want you to like it."

"I'm sure it'll be fine."

"I'm worried."

"How much more time do you need?"

"Like three minutes."

"Well, I guess we can stand this horrible fucking noise for three minutes," I said.

"I don't like discomfort."

I got off the stool. "You'll live."

"You are so blue collar,"she said jokingly.

"Oh, yeah."

"Yeah, only blue collar people say things like, 'you'll live.'"

"What do you usually do in this situation?"

"Bitch a lot."

"After when you're done bitching what happens then?"

"I get drunk until things make sense."

"Do you want to have my babies?"

She laughed and said, "I'm not ready to have kids."

"You're 32 years old."

"That doesn't mean I'm ready for that commitment yet."

"Norman Mailer had like six wives and eight kids."

"Norman Mailer was a Harvard grad, had money and you're a shiftless asshole."

"A lot of shiftless assholes have babies," I said.

"With shiftless women. I'm not a shiftless woman. I'm educated, I'll have a nice forty hour a week job soon that'll pay good money and give me health care. I'll be on my feet and living a good easy life here on the lower east side. You'll be in Ohio half starving, you're like some kind of martyr."

"I'm not a martyr," I said.

"You live in that town for what? I've read your memoir. You used to live out west, you used to go out and do things. It was so sad reading it, such a strong young man with courage and determination and slowly, gradually without you ever noticing it all went away."

"I lost several things."

"You didn't write what you lost."

"The memoir ended right before I lost them. I will have to write another memoir to record what I lost."

She handed me my eggs and veggies. She sat down next to me, smiled and said, "How many memoirs you going to write?"

"Simone De Beauvoir wrote four."

"She was a professor of philosophy who had lived through Nazi occupation and the creator of modern feminism, you're a cook at a restaurant in Ohio."

"I used to be a pizza boy."

"Yeah, and Celine was like a doctor and fought in World War 1."

"I haven't done anything."

We finished breakfast and I went in the bedroom to check Gmail. Desmond Tondo was on and decided to G-chat with me.

Desmond: You're in New York.

Me: Yeah. I'm getting my picture taken.

Desmond: That sounds good. Where are you going to be tonight?

Me: At the Opium Christmas party.

Desmond: Good, I'm going to be there.

Me: I gotta take a shower but I'll see you tonight.

Desmond: Sounds good.

Desmond Tondo was a writer. He was also a very strange person. He graduated from Harvard with an English degree and then decided to work in the hiring department of a hedge fund company. He was an attractive Italian man. He wasn't Ellis Island Italian, his family came later in the sixties. He had one book published about a suburban landscape catching on fire and turning suburbia into flames. He had grown up in suburbia in Connecticut. He found suburbia hell on the human soul. His parents had fallen for the advertisement that raising kids in suburbia with good schools and a high level of security would make their child an adult that would be efficient in the modern workforce. It was true, he was efficient, he had succeeded. He made good money and he was living out his conception of the good life. Desmond had a very well-ordered life. He went to work in the morning, he wrote four days a week, read a little every day and still had time to date women. He kept everything straight, clean, and organized. His face was shaved and he always smelled nice.

Last summer Desmond came to visit me for a few days. He didn't shave those days. He wore t-shirts with leather shoes. He came to write an article that appeared on the Huffington Post. Desmond and I drove around the Youngstown area for two days doing nothing. He was fascinated by the shittiness of it all. There were houses close together but it wasn't suburbs. It was summer and the poor blacks and whites were playing basketball on the streets. The crack heads were walking down the sidewalks. The old steel mills looked old and appalling. People were sitting on their porches drinking beer and swearing at each other. It was a very different scene.

At night we went to the local strip club where he would get dances from impoverished women that didn't even know what Harvard was. They assumed it was something only spoken of on television. He didn't have to play big shot. He didn't have to tell people what schools he went to, what hedge fund company he worked for, that he lived in Manhattan in a nice apartment. All those facts which are so crucial to life in New York City meant nothing in

Youngstown. He seemed very much at peace in Youngstown. He was dressed normally and had a courteous personality. Everyone accepted him as a person just walking around the earth.

Desmond liked sex though: he liked women. When he was at the strip joint he spent a lot of money on the dancers. The last time I was in New York a pretty girl didn't pass us without him making a comment. He told me he would spend money to go on boats where everyone was having swinger sex. He had a real passion for sex. The way DiMaggio had for baseball or Brando had for acting. He put his heart and soul in the getting of sex, into the things women require for a man to have sex with them. And I assume even though I've never experienced personally, he must have devoted a lot of heart into the act of sex.

15.

Petra and I were sitting on her bed saying nice things to each other. Things that people say to each other when they first meet and are having a very care-free good time. We were not serious. There was nothing serious about us. Soon I would be leaving. There was no reason for us to care about each other in any deep or meaningful way. We were nothing to each other. Two genitals that had showed up to fuck each other. Our relationship was like a roller coaster. We got on, we rode, we had fun, we got off. We were never going to be in-love. We were never going to get married and have children. I was never going to learn the most embarrassing moments of her childhood. She was never going to learn what hospital I was born in. We were never going to meet each other's parents. We would never drive across country together or visit Rome, standing together looking upon The Coliseum. We would never sit at a Waffle House, her eating a breakfast burrito, me a waffle and grits talking about the day's activities. Petra was from the south, but her Waffle House and grits days were over. She ate a lot of seaweed and rice. If she came to Youngstown she would view the people that surrounded me as sociological animals one looked down upon. I viewed them as sociological animals also, but they were my friends and enemies. An educated white collar person couldn't hate poor people, for they were screwed and disenfranchised and that's why they acted like that. They could do that because they didn't have to be around them. They could leave and go back to their suburban neighborhood and white collar job. I couldn't afford those feelings. I was surrounded by them, I worked with them, I was one of them. My private life was that of literature and philosophy. In the privacy of my own home I would read and write things. But my public life was that of a stumble bum working at cheap labor jobs swearing and not shaving every morning like everyone else.

When I got my first book published six years ago before sitting with Petra people thought I would eventually pick up and go to New York City and try to become a writer. I had thought that myself. I had traveled out west, I had lived in several different states before the age of 23. States as far away from Ohio as Oregon and California. New York City was only six hours away from Youngstown. When looking back on it, perhaps I should have left to New York City. I would have been surrounded by writers. I would have been doing readings and making connections. It was logical if I wanted to become a writer. I was scared though: scared of not being smart enough, of not being good enough. I was just a little boy from Ohio, I wasn't a rich kid who had been to an ivy league college. I was no one. I was a butcher's son, a factory worker's son. I was a child of the Rust Belt. Came from blue collar lands. I was so full of dreams when I was young, I was going to go to New York City and shock everyone. I was going to make them believe that blue collar people could think and write. I didn't though. I never had the courage. I didn't go to college for years. Instead of preparing to get that intelligent and aware of my world, I sat in in my house and read Wittgenstein alone.

When people in New York City or online would tell me what good college they went to or what their parents did. I felt little. I felt out of place. It was not my world. I felt like I didn't have a right to be there talking to them. I didn't belong. It was not my world, it was theirs. I was merely a guest. In Ohio I felt like a person, a participant in events. I was of Youngstown, I could say with pride, "My mother worked for GM." I could say my name was Baradat, and I was related to the people who owned Baradat's Market and they would say they used to shop there and they loved their pigs in the blanket. I had a link to the land. I was anchored, I was a citizen in Youngstown. In New York City I was a subject. I received privileges from the white collar literary world, not rights.

Petra's cell phone rang, she picked it up and looked at the number and said, "It's John Walters. It's for you." She handed me the phone.

I pressed down on the little rubber bottom and said, "Hello, John."

"Benny."

"Yes."

"The shoot is tonight at Hu's apartment in Bushwick."

"How long is it?"

"Three hours."

"That's a long time," I said.

"It's only fucking three hours. You can do it."

"I don't know if I can do anything," I said.

"I'm sure you'll survive."

"Okay, what time is it?"

"6 p.m."

"Okay."

"We have to do an interview after. There's going to be two people with cameras, and then we are supposed to meet someone after to do the interview."

"Okay, that sounds good."

"All right, can you handle that?"

"I can handle it."

"Let me talk to Petra for a minute."

I handed the cell phone to Petra.

John Walters was a young man, around 19 or 20 from Philadelphia. He was of working class background also. He had spent his high school years reading Lydia Davis and Lorrie Moore and I assume feeling terrible in his bedroom. He had a lot of emotion and a complete disdain for anything serious. He worked as a dog walker and a personal assistant to a woman from Kansas who had a trust fund. The woman from Kansas did nothing all day but write silly articles for lame magazines and talk out her ass. He would get her coffee and sushi for a high price. The woman acted like it was a privilege to serve her. John Walters didn't go to college. He didn't go because nothing really mattered to him. Suicide seemed for him so imminent no one even suggested that he attend. Everyone was waiting for him to kill himself. He wore outfits from the thrift store. The outfits were all appalling. He was overall a very appalling individual. On his blog there were many photos of Fran Drescher looking sexy. Unintelligent vulgar people assume movies with cannibals eating people or adults having sex with minors was shocking. But John Walters knew what shocking really was, it was things like Fran Drescher. That American society had allowed people like her and Tom Cruise to ever become famous. For they wouldn't have become famous and influences on our society if there wasn't something heinous about the culture itself. He enjoyed showing people how truly sick they were. How they worshiped the sexiness of Fran Drescher. The question that John Walters posed to everyone he met was, "Why do anything if the apex of human development is Fran Drescher?" There was something godless and conquering about John Walters. He was not going to sit with you and quietly discuss the Supreme Court decisions leading up to Roe v. Wade or Talcott Parsons but he would make an impression. He was the living embodiment of America. His family had been for years and were real Americans. Hu Chin was a first generation immigrant, I was a third, Petra was a first, but John Walter's history goes deep into the history of America. His family

103

had come over in the 1700s. They were Protestants from England. His ancestors had fought in the Revolutionary War, the War of 1812, they fought the Indians, they fought in the Civil War, World War 1 and 2 and lived through The Great Depression. He was firmly placed in this land. He was a product of 300 years of American sociology. He was loud and conquering.

16.

Petra and I screwed all that day. We went to Rockefeller Center and looked at the ice skaters. It cost too much to ice skate so we just took pictures. We went to a bakery and the post office. We made jokes, laughed and touched each other. We didn't grope. We were too professional and well-ordered for public displays of affection.

Night came and snow started to fall on New York City. It was pretty. I liked coming out of the subway into Brooklyn to see snow falling. New York City was always better in the winter. Everyone had their nice coats and hats on. People had expensive gloves on. Everyone looked normal and okay. In the summer New York City looks like hell. There is something horrible about seeing a lot of rich people sweat.

We got to Hu Chin's apartment in Bushwick. His apartment was above a jewelry shop. Petra and I couldn't find the door. We went in the shop and asked the old man at the counter where the door was. He said go outside and turn left. We did. The door was there. We buzzed and were let in.

The hallway was ugly and had bad lighting. We went upstairs to his door. Hu Chin opened the door and let us in. Hu Chin was short and frail. He was only 5 and a half feet tall and weighed less than 130 pounds. He smiled and went back to organizing the photo shoot. Hu Chin was a first generation immigrant from Taiwan. He was very much a product of the Asian work ethic. He worked endlessly on his writing and on promoting himself. He had no close friends and no lovers. He got up everyday and worked. He had no religion, there was no supernatural reality for him. Life was very concrete for Hu. He was a mixture of Confucius and Buddha. The Confucius was all about work, morals and duty. The Buddhist part was seeing that everything would pass and there was no reason to cling to anything too strongly. Work was the only thing that held him together. Women would pass, his parents moved back to Taiwan, everything eventually left, but the work. Even the books passed. One book was finished and he was on to another one. The work kept him alive, even if everything left he would still have his work. He liked the Protestant philosophers Kant and Schopenhauer, their views on duties, imperatives, suffering and music. Hu Chin believed firmly in self-control and rational action. His life was well-ordered, organized, and perfected. There was little freedom in his everyday life, when spending time with him, one could tell he was thinking three moves ahead. There was none of that American spontaneity and the spirit of the old blues man about him. He didn't smoke, drink much, or have sex with women after his readings. But when he wrote freedom came. His stories and poems were always fucked up and completely out of tune with his Confucius/German Philosopher way of life he was leading in public. His stories were always strange, featuring talking animals and humiliating experiences, but one could still see that work ethic. The stories were always well-ordered, perfected, pondered over intensely. He would sit in front of the computer and dwell over the sentences, making sure they conveyed exactly what he wanted them to. There was no joking around when it came to him building a sentence. It was deadly serious. He enjoyed the freedom to control the sentences. A person could never fully control their public life. We are always subject to the contingencies of others and nature. But when writing poetry or fiction, a person may assume the role of boss and dictator over the story and style. There is freedom in literature. In science and engineering one has to get to a certain fact that society wants. Society wants a car that runs on less gas, the engineers must design that car, society wants a pill that makes their dicks hard, the scientist must get to that certain fact. Society does not demand certain facts from its story tellers. The story tellers still remain free to make their stories. Hu Chin's behaviors could have been conducive to science, but he didn't want to seek certain facts. But there is something of the doctor and scientist in the writer. Fans are more than just people out there buying units, they are patients coming to you for therapy. A writer knows this because he or she has gone to many writers and asked for therapy before they ever started writing. Romance writers know the people who buy their books are those who lack good sex lives and are coming to get mental escape, horror novelists know that their readers are scared of real things, be it bills or losing their jobs, and have come to get escape. Writers of literature, if they are real writers, know that their readers are confused about reality and the emotions derived from that reality and are looking for clarity concerning the life that they are engulfed in.

Two years before in the summer I sat with Hu on the roof of his apartment building. He lived in a different apartment then. He lived with four other men who he never spoke to. We sat on his roof for several hours talking about what ever came to us. He kept pretending that he would jump off the roof. I kept yelling to get away from the edge and that they would blame it on me and send me to prison. Eventually we got tired and went back to his closet room. It must have been 8 feet long and 5 feet wide. I sat down and took my shoes off. I had forgotten to put socks on and my feet smelled badly. It was a horrible smell, it was unbearable. There we were two writers, earlier in the day an Irish immigrant had declared us two of the best writers of our generation and all we could think about was how to get my feet to stop stinking.

I went to the bathroom and washed them off with his gay roommate's expensive shampoo. The smell went away a little. I went back in the small closet room and Hu sprayed female body spray on my feet. My feet smelled like watermelon. The whole thing was very strange considering there was a giant bear head in the corner of the room staring at us. I laid down on the floor and went to sleep. In the morning he made me a vegan smoothie that was purple.

While watching him walking around the room making sure the two women from the magazine were well taken care of and that everything was going smoothly. I looked at him and his tense face hoping one day he would get enough money writing and move out west and farm corn or beans. Or maybe he would move to a small town in Pennsylvania and play drums and relax. He probably never would though: work was his life. He was one of those people that died as soon as they stopped working.

John Walters was there, he was sitting outside on the fire escape smoking and drinking Pabst. He was acting carefree and totally apathetic to the world around him. Jason Bassini, a writer from Seattle who had grown up in Utah was sitting on a stool drinking a beer. I went over to him and gave him a huge hug. We had spoken many times on Gmail chat. He was twenty-four and had graduated college two years before with a Psychology degree. He was short, very thin and Italian looking. Actually all the males were very skinny. I was the largest by a good fifty pounds. Jason was from a different place than Hu, John and I. He was from the west. He was from the deserts of Utah and the forests of Washington. He had grown up under big skies like Tom White. He had grown up amongst natural wonders, Mexicans, and Navajos.

Jason went to Catholic School when he was little. Jason Bassini was the only one of us raised with any religion. He never wrote or spoke about religion. There was no god for him. When he was bored, once every six months he would attend afternoon mass by himself. He would sit and kneel with the Latinos in Seattle saying his Hail Marys. He considered it a nice thing to do when he was really bored. You go some place and perform an ancient ritual with people you don't know. Even though he didn't believe in god, Catholic mass seemed more worthwhile than Wal-Mart or Starbucks.

Jason's parents were both high level executives. He told me that one night on Gmail chat, "My parents are high level executives."

I googled "high level executives." It didn't supply any real information. Both of his parents were professional people that wanted him to be a professional person. Jason Bassini finished college by the time he was 22. He was showing signs of being a professional human being. His dad got him a job at his company writing for reality television in Seattle. Jason went there and didn't care. He left the job and started working in an office writing directions on how to work things. He sat for eight hours a day staring at a computer checking Facebook and writing long emails to a girl in Munich. None of the success and good things of life made him happy. He left there and got a job working at a coffee house. He rejected his parents by not taking part in the ambition game the corporate world supplies.

Jason seemed really nervous. He seemed absolutely terrified, but it didn't seem like he was terrified at what was going on in the apartment. It seemed like that was his natural demeanor, that of being terrified.

The other people in the room were the two photographers. I shook their hands and they told me their names. They had common names like Sarah and Jen. They told us that they were doing it for free. That they had to take photos like this of jackass writers to build a resume so that one day they could get a real job photographing the Mayor of New York or Tom Cruise. They didn't talk much.

Two women sat in the room. One was a pretty Asian girl who was supposed to be a girl named Charlotte Chofu. Charlotte Chofu was a writer from South Carolina that Hu had made friends with. I had never read her writing. Charlotte couldn't show up so Hu got a stand in. There was also another stand in, a little white girl wearing a Burger King shirt. She was standing in for Leslie Heaney. Leslie was in the mental ward for bi-polar disorder. According to Hu she was walking down the street in Williamsburg, crying, talking to invisible people. She kept saying things that did not correspond with reality and everyone became worried. Leslie got on a bus and went back to her hometown in Pennsylvania and the voices did not stop. Her parents brought her to the mental ward three weeks earlier. She was cutting herself and screaming at everyone about how much they suck. Everyone assumed they didn't suck and that she was nuts. In the mental ward they gave her medication which took the voices away. Leslie was a great writer and person. Her mind was quick and decisive. She was half black and half Irish but looked completely white with bright red hair. But strangely she had no freckles, her lips were full, and her behind was very pronounced. She wrote poems about emotional collapse. She was in a constant state of emotional collapse. She was not comfortable on the planet earth.

Leslie Heaney's stand-in had something wrong with her. Her hair was matted, her face was in a constant snarl and she seemed like she might have a pill addiction. She was from Queens and had found John Walters on the Internet. No one told me either of the stand-ins' real names. No one told the photographers that the two women were not the actual women they were supposed to be photographing. The Asian woman was very nice and responsible. She took being somebody else for the sake of a prank seriously. The little white girl made funny comments and looked like she wanted to lay down.

Petra stood behind the kitchen counter drinking a beer video taping everything. She liked being there, it was a real New York scene. There was photographers, writers, and pretty people.

There was a lot of ego in the room. Hu, Jason, John and I were that kid in high school and in our hometowns who were the smartest. We weren't the best at math or valedictorians, but we were that person and most of the time the only person that recognized how absurd everything was. How irrational modern living really is. We were all very lonely people. We had no connection to the mainstream, to the realities of people consumed with television, sports, the purchasing of expensive products for the sake of telling people the price, ambition without reason. Our alienation even went to the lower classes, none of us went to prison, none of us did hard drugs, none of us cared about what other people did. We were on the outside, we weren't looking in. But to get things in life, like food, shelter, and bank accounts you have to go into society and you have to deal with those who belong to the mainstream. All of it seemed unbearable to us. From the lowest crack head to the head of corporations. You were born one day, from some random person living in some random place, you grew in a certain location with that woman and sometimes a man telling you how to live, you get to school and they teach you math, how to read, some history and civics. The television notifies you what to wear and eat. You have indoor heating and plumbing. Nothing happens. Nothing is exciting at all. You go to Olive Garden and peacefully eat your food. You go to Disney Land and everything is clean and nice. You watch *Smokey and The Bandit* on a lazy

Saturday afternoon. You play hide and go seek with your neighbors. Nobody fights, nobody kills each other. Nobody asks you to do anything. There's a lot of food and if you don't have any money the government will give you a food card. In the summer you ride bikes with your friends around the neighborhood. You ride down to the pharmacy and pick up candy and baseball cards. You make ramps made out of discarded wood and jump the ramps. You get a little older and smoke weed in your friend's basement. It seems exciting for awhile but it fades. You find somebody to have sex with, you lose your virginity, you eventually find out that your sex life will never match the sex that takes place on the Internet. You realize that serial monogamy is your destiny and that makes things even more boring. You graduate high school and they notify you that you must find a place in the modern economy. The modern economy offers a limitless amount of jobs that are boring. All the jobs are boring from construction worker to office worker to lawyer. Some make more money than others, you assume if you make more money perhaps you will be able to purchase excitement. You purchase a vacation to the Rocky Mountains but then you realize that the original Europeans who went to the Rocky Mountains got there in wagons which took months and while they were traveling they had to fight Indians, kill their own food and search for water. You did it in a car in two days and fought no Indians. You start to become overwhelmed with the nothingness. You realize the purpose of alcohol. You spend your days reading Richard Yates instead of trying to make friends and do anything constructive with your life. You eventually end up in New York City with other like-minded individuals living a generalized meaningless of trying to pass the time while nothing happens.

The two photographers had all of us sit on a couch. We all sat together peacefully and responsibly at first. It looked kind of like a family photo. Everyone thought that was boring, which was predictable. So the photographers had us sit on the couch with the men touching and having their legs overlap. John Walters and I kept pretending we were homosexuals in the photos which entertained everyone. Nobody thought it was homophobic because both of us have had sex with men when we were bored and lonely at different points in our lives.

We took a break, so Jason Bassini and I went on the fire escape to smoke. It was dark and we could see Brooklyn and the lights of Manhattan in the distance. Snow was falling but it wasn't a bad temperature. Jason looked short, frail and nervous.

I said, "You took a plane out here?"

"Yeah, it was only three hundred dollars."

"That's not bad."

"No."

We stood in silence and looked at the snow for a minute and I said, "Where do you work now?"

"At a coffee shop that serves barbecue."

"People eat ribs and drink espressos at the same time."

"No, people come in there and wonder what the fuck is going on."

"That sounds dumb, what do you do there?"

"I work the register and make coffee."

"They don't have you make ribs."

"No, they have Mexicans that do that," said Jason.

"Are you going to move here?"

"I think about it, but I don't feel like trying to raise enough cash every month to live here. Every thing is fucking expensive."

"Supply and demand. Everyone wants to live here. This is one of the few places in America you can work for television, make movies, be a writer, a stock broker and walk dogs and get paid for it."

"I've never done anything like this."

"Like what?" I said.

"Get my picture taken for a magazine."

"No, this is very unusual. I feel like Britney Spears."

"Are we Britney Spears?"

"I think we are now."

"Are we famous now?" Jason said.

"What does that mean to be famous?"

"I think it means, hmm, that people notice you. You are like walking down the street and people are like, 'look, that's so and so.'"

"I don't know if we'll achieve that level with this magazine."

"The magazine is pretty big."

"I've never heard of it. I was in a music magazine in England and it didn't cause any sales."

"You don't think it will cause sales."

"The only thing that causes real sales is if you are on the tables at Barnes and Nobles and Borders," I said.

"I don't think my writing will land on those tables."

"Neither will mine. I don't think it matters, though: I mean, from writing I've released a lot of emotions. People send me emails telling me that it entertained them. I've met people like you and the other people in there. When I come to New York City people buy my meals and beer. I mean, for a fuckass from Youngstown, that's pretty cool."

"It never occurred to me to be a big writer. When I was in high school I remember really liking the story of Emily Dickinson. I didn't care much for her poetry. It was all right, whatever, Emily Dickinson. But I remember walking around my neighborhood thinking about Emily Dickinson walking around lonely in her house. Nobody was around. She was wearing white walking around her garden being scared and nervous about everything. I always imagined her sitting outside looking at a slug slowly making its way somewhere. She had the time to watch the whole thing, so she did. She would watch caterpillars and when a mosquito landed on her arm she wouldn't kill it. She would stare at it instead in wonder. I would ride my bike into the woods and be alone and stare at things pretending I was Emily Dickinson. Sometimes I would imagine Emily Dickinson was hanging out with me. I would think if Emily Dickinson only met me, she would have had a friend. I didn't think that about Stephen King. I didn't imagine I was attending a movie premier of my book, or doing long signing tours across the world."

"I liked Emily Dickinson too. I read everything by Kerouac in high school. I liked the idea of a man traveling around working odd jobs and having relationships with random women. I liked that even though he never got money for writing until the end, he wrote all those books without ever considering he would get famous. He just wrote without concern for anyone. It was like a hobby, that was all. I mean, now, I don't even read his writing anymore. It all seems disjointed and sloppy at times and I've realized I'm not that kind of person. I'm not the kind of person that goes out drinking every night. Hell, I barely drink at all, this is the first I've drank in three weeks. I don't like drugs. I don't even think people should do drugs. I don't even think weed should be legalized. I like to travel but I don't sleep in my car. I get hotel rooms or sleep in well-ordered camp grounds in a nice new tent. I'm not like those old school writers like Hemingway or Pound who traveled all over the world and lived sweet lives. America has two wars right now, I haven't attempted to join the military. I don't care about fighting in a war, I don't find wars sentimental or romantic. Maybe they were back then, who the fuck knows, but right now the military seems like a giant corporation that requires a lot of exercise. I like comfort, I'm used to it. I like security and for things to be normal. I mean it, it isn't like philosophical. I don't have any philosophical Kantian reasons for these feelings. These are just reflexes. I grew up in a normal little house on 5 acres of land in a rural part of Ohio. But it wasn't like we were in the country. I was ten minutes from a city with malls and shopping outlets. We had indoor plumbing and heating. My parents made enough money I never had to worry about lacking the necessities of life. I could say philosophically that it would be better for Americans to put down their cars and their excess and go back to the land, of outhouses and fireplaces. But I don't want that. I don't even know what that is. I don't know how to live a simple life. I like to go to work and go back to my house and check my email, turn on the lights at night and read a book. I like being warm in the winter. I don't even like working odd jobs. I didn't mind sweeping floors and doing stupid shit before. But now, I'm getting older and want to be respected and have some sort of authority in the world. I don't really care about impressing other people. But I don't feel like being shit on by idiot managers anymore. I think that is why I started reading Richard Wright and Richard Yates. Their characters are always trapped in the modern economy. Beatnik characters never have to work, they are always out, running around, having a good time. Even Bukowski is like that, his characters do work. But they are always having a good time also. I hardly ever have a good time."

"Neither do I."

Jason and I crawled through the window into the room. The photographers were taking single pictures of us. Everyone stood around and waited for their turn. John got his picture taken first. He stood smiling a huge goofy smile. He looked like a maniac. Then they went to the two girls I didn't know. The little white girl snarled and the Asian girl gave a pretty smile. Hu went and did funny things and made the girls laugh. I went next and pretended I was nervous and weird like I didn't want my picture taken. The photographers smiled at me to show that it was okay. I walked away and Jason went. He looked absolutely fucked but they took his picture anyway.

During all this Petra was taping it with her digital camera. It was very important that it was documented on digital film. She said she planned on putting it on Youtube.

The photographers put their stuff away. Hu, Jason and John looked on the Internet for stuff that didn't matter to me. I walked over once, looked and didn't care. I went back to the couch, sat down and drank a beer. Hu Chin's apartment was very bare. Nothing was on the walls. The walls badly needed painted. There was no carpet. The kitchen was small, the oven and refrigerator were old and ramshackle. His bedroom was a lonely little place with books on the floor stacked very orderly. Hu Chin lived with another writer named David Lexmark. David Lexmark wrote articles for *The Believer* and got his stories in popular hipster magazines. He had gone to a prestigious MFA program, attended a shitload of writer's workshops, and now taught English composition classes at a local NYC university. David was obsessed with new writers and reading all of their books. The man was on top of it. He had ambition and the will to succeed in the world of NYC literature. David Lexmark was always very outgoing, courteous and charming. He never frowned or acted weird or considered suicide. He wasn't that type of person. Hu Chin lived with that person.

Hu Chin kept talking on his cell phone, trying to arrange a meeting place with the woman who was supposed to be interviewing us. Her name was Margo. No one told me her last name. I didn't want to be interviewed by anyone named Margo. But they notified me it was my destiny. I liked email interviews, the person sent me the questions and I answered them slowly taking my time. Doing things in person, with people, I did not enjoy.

Everyone finished their beers and we left. They told me we had to go to Manhattan, which meant more subway.

17.

We were all on the subway. There were no subways in Youngstown. Getting on a little train underground seemed absurd to me. In Ohio you drive cars and buy gas. No one owns a car in New York City. They don't pay car insurance or buy gas. They buy Metro Cards. Petra sat next to me. We sat close. But we didn't kiss or hold hands. We didn't show any physical affection for each other. I was never the type of person that was wild and showed sexual affection in public. I never jumped out of planes or scaled cliff walls. I was boring. I was a little minuscule man that sat in his house and read books. Petra knew that. Why she would enjoy being around such a boring man, confused me. Petra and I didn't talk on the subway. There was nothing to say. Jason hung on to a pole and said nothing either, he was as confused by the subway as I was. There were people everywhere. None of them speaking to each other. There was no community in New York City. Half of the people in New York City at any given time weren't actually New Yorkers. The only real New Yorker I had encountered on this trip was the little white girl pretending she was Leslie Heaney. Nobody was an actual New Yorker. Nobody on the subway cared about each other. Everyone was a nonhuman machine to each other. Each traveling to a destination that didn't matter to the other person. It was completely alienating and frustrating as a human to live through such an experience. To be surrounded by so many other people and not to care about any of them. New York was a strange place. Over 8 million people living together in close proximity. Ohio only had 11 million and that was over a much wider space. There were 250,000 in ancient Athens, and ancient Rome at the height of its power had a population of 500,000. The people of Athens and Rome were alienated and emotionally disfigured with much smaller populations. Athens and Rome were much different though: or not really. Instead of slaves titled slaves New York had Mexicans titled cheap labor employees. Instead of disenfranchised workers New York had Harlem, Bushwick and Queens. Instead of drunken symposiums out in the open sunshine, New York had drunken symposiums in bars with expensive liquor. Unlike the ancient cities that grew their food right outside the city walls with slave labor. New York City ships their food in from all over the world and gets all its oil and natural gas from thousands of miles away. Instead of Socrates being a blacksmith, it was an economist named Paul Krugman who graduated from MIT. No one in the city produced anything, everyone was living off the entertainment and finance sectors. You either met someone who worked for a television station, a publisher or magazine. Or you met someone who did IT for Morgan Stanley, did accounting for CitiBank, or worked on Wall Street. Or you met people that walked their dogs, cooked their food at fancy restaurants and cleaned their houses. It was a strange way of life to me. I was from Ohio where there were factories where people worked building products. I grew up around farms that were producing food. There were natural gas wells with people working on them all over the area. There were no offices in Youngstown. Everyone was producing and working to survive. People from Youngstown referred to writers and office workers people who, "sit on their butts." I was on the subway surrounded by people who, "sit on their butts." I was terribly conflicted about who I was: I could see Amanda's father Charlie working ten hours standing up working a press, pumping out parts sweating in a 120 degree factory in the summer. There was my brother who drove truck twelve hours at a time trying to make money. There were my friends who had done construction and helped build houses with the strength of their bodies. There were all the strippers, landscapers, and dishwashers, all there in my mind, with their strong bodies, working, and struggling for money. There was my father who carried huge cow carcasses from meat lockers to the cutting table, with his arms bulging and his face wincing. There was my mother working in the GM plant for 33 years. The people on the subway were not my people. I felt no hostility towards them. They had grown up somewhere different, with a different set of labor and world views offered to them. They had to take it. I had to take mine. It was our fate.

18.

We got off the subway in Manhattan. It was back to giant buildings and people walking every where. We walked around the lower east side looking for a bookstore. Hu Chin had lived in New York City for seven years now and he was leading. I was following behind talking to Jason about writing. John was talking to Petra. They seemed to get along. They were talking, their mouths were moving, words were coming out, they were sporadically laughing, they seemed happy. I was talking to Jason, we weren't laughing. Jason talked about a vampire story I wrote and how it was cohesive and made sense. How he was surprised that I would write something that made sense. I told him I made sense now. He told me he still didn't make sense so he was writing poetry. I told him he would make sense one day. He said he was unsure that he would ever make sense. I said it would happen. He wasn't sure. I said he would get older and time would pass, things would pass, and he would realize that things passed, and it was all right, but sad. He said things had passed for him. I said more things would pass, but they would take longer to pass and he would be surprised how long it took and that you didn't even notice you were involved in something to begin with. I said that life and people mutate. You don't get more intelligent by getting older. Life doesn't progress. It doesn't start at one point and end up at victory. There was no victory. There were mutations. Little dialectic mutations of things turning into other things over long spans of time. History does not have attention deficit disorder. It is a slow grinding process, everything gradually coming to terms with new things, changing along with them, to the point we don't even notice it. He said 9-11 broke that rule. I said 8 years have passed. We have internalized it now. I said humans weren't fixed. We aren't alone either. We may feel alone at times. But we aren't. We are very dependent upon each other. You might go in your room, listen to sad music and cry while reading a book, but someone is out there supplying the electricity for you to do that, growing the food, shipping the food, for you to keep eating, so you can keep being sad. You have to work, you depend on owners, stock markets and all those little dirty stock brokers, you depend on truck drivers, construction workers, marketers to sell the products that keeps your job alive, you depend on doctors and nurses, you depend on schools teaching children, we depend on government even though we enjoy bitching about them, we love police, courts, prisons, laws, lawyers, and legislation. We are a dependent species, at the mercy of each other. I asked him if he had ever studied political statistics. He said no. I told him that what politicians look at are graphs with little dots, boxes and lines everywhere, symbolizing our wants and needs. Humanity is a bunch of particles, mutating endlessly, bouncing into each other, each particle with their own wants and needs, but there are other particles, with the same exact wants and needs, and those particles are the same as you, and there are other particles with different wants and needs, and those are the other particles, some particles have this and some have that, and some particles have nothing. And they flow around the charts, going in and out of the boxes, making one bar higher than another, filling up one slice of the pie and making another slice smaller. Yes, you are condemned personally to take responsibility and make something of the life you've been given, but at the same time in the grand scheme of things you're a particle on a graph somewhere, being stared at and studied, with researchers in little offices making critical judgments on what these particles are doing and want. Jason said he felt like a particle. I said worse things have happened. He said that's true.

We got to the bookstore. Margo wasn't there. There was some sort of speech being given by an author of a book about military contracts. She stated that George W. Bush ruined America and had given military contracts out to all of his friends. That Bush was obsessed with giving federal tax money to his buddies. The worst thing was that the tax money didn't even exist. He actually took out loans to give money to his friends. Everyone was very happy to be shitting on Bush. Bush was a good person to hate. He was Republican, he was from Texas, he was white, he went to Harvard, he talked funny, he mispronounced words, he enjoyed baseball and golf, he hardly ever did anything right, he was completely human except for the Harvard thing. Jason and I went outside and stood on the sidewalk. It was cold and snow was falling. I said to Jason that I thought Bush was just the end result of Reagan and Clinton excess. Everybody had money and it made them apathetic and decadent and everybody seemed fine with it. Everyone played along. And this guy shows up, the king of decadence and nihilism, George W. Bush. And everyone was like, okay, whatever. Because they were just as decadent and nihilistic. Jason said that Clinton didn't do anything about the stock markets, Clinton didn't care about regulating anything. All he did was get his dick sucked and tell wonderful stories about Arkansas. I said people act like this is something new. It started with Reagan, the banks became deregulated, everyone started dreaming up dreams that weren't based in reality. They took out loans instead of worked. They got credit cards instead of saved. There was no long term thinking, no long term sense of justice.

Hu Chin came out of the bookstore and said Margo would meet us at Petra's apartment. Petra's apartment was several blocks away. We walked down the street. John Walters came over to me and said, "Are you fucking Petra?"

"I don't know," I said.

"That means you are."

"It might mean that."

"I have a Japanese girlfriend."

"Oh yeah?" I said.

"Yeah, I keep living with her, and we keep arguing and we call that our life together. One time I sat in a chair drunk in the living room and yelled for 45 minutes about stuff I can't remember. Then she came over and punched me in the face."

"That sounds romantic."

"It was. She reminds me of Mom."

19.

We got to Petra's apartment. Everyone found seats in the kitchen. I remained standing. Petra opened a bottle of cheap wine. John Walters drank a huge glass of it. I sipped on it. It was red and tasted like piss.

Petra turned her iPod stereo thing on. It played indie bands the normal population of humans would never have recognized.

Margo arrived. She was a white woman wearing a nice coat. Her face was pale with brown hair. I didn't trust her. She wrote for a major corporate magazine making decent money. She was just starting out. Her article was to interview some unknown writers. The magazine she worked for interviewed such people as Scarlet Johansson and Rhianna. Margo was young though: still in her late twenties. In her thirties after years of doing the right things and paying attention to detail and showing up on time they would allow her to interview whoever was famous in 2016. Margo had goals. She had always had goals. She went to a nice Catholic school and then went to college at Columbia for journalism. She worked hard, got mostly As except for math class which she got a C, and her Modern biology class which she got a B. But for the most part her academic record was perfect. At school she made connections, she made friends with professors that wrote her wonderful recommendations. She did community service and in her senior year won an award for journalism. She did an internship at the New York Times, doing mindless stupid things for the journalists. But she did them with pride and precision. Margo was a hard worker. She believed in corporate media.

Margo grew up in a nice community in Connecticut. Her parents got divorced when she was 12. Her dad went across town and she lived with her mother. Her dad was busy with work. And her mother was busy with work. Margo had a lot of time alone because her parents wouldn't let her play sports because they thought sports were dangerous and she should be studying. When Margo graduated from high school her parents bought her a new car. Margo hugged her father and Margo's father paid the bills on the car. Nobody was really happy at Margo's house. Margo would come in after school, her mother would be working at a computer. Her mother would say hi, how are you, Margo would say something and that was it. Margo would go to her room and write or read and listen to indie music. When Margo would visit her dad, her dad would be working at a computer and really no talking took place. Nobody believed in religion, witchcraft or even sports. Everyone just worked all the time making money and maintaining a very successful life. Margo's parents would go out with their friends sometimes. They would go to lunch or dinner at a nice clean restaurant. Everything was very organized, the conversation went easily, nothing serious was discussed, only moderate complaining and some discussion of the kids. Margo's mother would find a boyfriend through an online dating site. She would date the guy for six months and then break up. There was never any real reason for the break up, they would just break up out of boredom. Margo's father dated a woman from his office for several years. Margo would come home and they would be sitting on the couch watching television together. Margo would look at them, feel bored and go to her room. There were no family activities. Margo's relatives lived out of state. When her parents graduated from college, they took the first jobs that were offered that paid the most and went to Connecticut. Margo never got to know her grandparents or cousins. During Christmas time and sometimes in the summer she would visit her relatives, but it meant nothing. Everyone would ask what she had been doing for the last six months. She would tell them her accomplishments and that was it. Margo had no sense of community. She lived in a neighborhood but no one spoke to each other. There was a neighbor girl who lived down the street she hung out with when she was little. But they haven't spoken in years. They were Facebook friends though. Most of the neighbors she had she didn't even know. She would see them mowing their grass or getting the mail but she never spoke to them and they never spoke to her. Margo never did yard work with her parents. Her father would mow the grass and weed whack himself without ever asking her to help and her mother paid landscapers to come and do the work. When something broke in her house her parents never fixed it themselves, instead they would pay someone to come and fix the water heater or furnace. When the car broke, they paid someone to fix it. There was no father and daughter out in the driveway with their hands covered in grease trying to fix the water pump. Margo's mother rarely ever cooked. Most of the time she would order out or stop somewhere and get something. There was no mother and daughter cooking together. Her mother did not teach her the family recipes. Margo had no ethnic heritage. She was white. Her family had come over several hundred years ago and all the traditions of the old country had been lost. She knew she was predominately Hungarian which explained her height and bulbous butt. But she had no love for cabbage soup and chicken paprikas.

Margo sat down on the futon. Petra handed her a glass of wine. Margo looked nervous. She had a strange job. Her job was to go to places and rooms she had never been, sit in them, and interview people she had never met before. She was surrounded by four very weird writers and a very weird girlfriend of a writer. She was seeing a 19 year old white kid who seemed on the verge of public suicide. A small unkempt nervous man from out west who seemed like he might commit a very disorderly suicide. A small Asian man who seemed very well-ordered and that one day he would commit a very well-ordered suicide. Myself, a bulky man with uncombed hair and indifferent eyes from Ohio who seemed like he might commit a very tragic suicide involving a large shotgun. And a half Asian woman who looked Native American drunk off of wine who seemed like she might a commit suicide while in a drunken stupor.

Margo, the hard worker with dreams was faced with people who lacked ambition and would probably all end in suicide. Margo felt like she was in the mental ward interviewing patients. She didn't seem happy. She knew she was doing it for her job. They were supplying payment and if she did a good job it would be good for further advancement. Hu, Jason and I considered it important that we try our best because it meant we would become more famous and get more readers. John Walters didn't seem to care at all.

Margo commenced the interview: she asked simple questions about the press, the writing, the writers and other things.

Hu Chin gave very well-ordered answers to her questions.

Jason gave personal answers, he seemed really nervous, like he wanted to do it but at the same time didn't know how.

I gave long dumb answers full of intellectual crap that could never be used in the magazine.

John Walters started talking about how he was going to move back to Philadelphia and live in a small room in his dad's house and write five line poems about sandwiches and Formica. He said he was going to break up with his girlfriend because he was bored and preferred to spend his time with Hart Crane poems. He then admitted that he didn't know who Hart Crane was but he did know he killed himself and he liked to read the poems of people who had killed themselves. Jason mentioned Plath had killed herself. Everyone in the room had read *The Bell Jar*. We all agreed *The Bell Jar* was very good. Half of us liked Plath's poetry and the other half didn't.

She asked Jason what he did, Jason said, "I have a psychology degree and work at a coffee shop that serves barbecue."

Everyone had a funny look on their face for a second and Margo said, "They serve barbecue?"

"Yes," said Jason.

"Like ribs and chicken wings with espressos and mochas?"

Then John Walters yelled, "GIVE ME SOME RIBS, RANCH WINGS, AND A ICED MOCHA WITH A SHOT OF EXPRESO RIGHT NOW, BITCH!"

Everyone laughed.

I said, "How does a barbecue coffee shop do?"

Jason said, "Not so good. People are usually confused."

"Every year where I live they have a thing called The Rib Cookoff. REO Speedwagon comes and plays a reunion concert and its fucking sweet," I said.

Margo said, "What was REO Speedwagon's famous song?"

John Walters yelled, "Can't Fight this Feeling. Goddamn great song to fuck your bitch to."

Walters was starting to feel the wine pretty good.

Margo asked Hu Chin about the press he was starting. Hu stood there nervous for a second and said, "It is going to be like offset."

Margo looked confused and said, "Offset?"

"Yeah, as opposed to POD."

"What's POD?"

"Print on Demand. Like books that only get a run of two to five hundred. We are going to print out like two thousand. And they will be offset and really nice."

Margo said, "What's the difference between an offset book and a POD book in quality?"

I said, "A lot of reviewers won't review POD."

Margo said, "You can tell when it is POD?"

"Yeah," Hu said.

I told Petra, "Go get a copy of my second book from your bedroom."

Petra came back with my second book and a nice book produced by Random House. Margo inspected them like a scientist and understood.

Our answers weren't very good. We weren't very awesome people. We were very unique, strange, and creative. But we weren't attractive and had not lived sweet lives of world travel and ivy league schools. Hu and Jason had cute faces but they were very short in person. In America a man can't be officially attractive unless he is at least 5-10. I remembered watching interviews of Dave Eggers on Youtube. He stood there beautiful, articulating wonderful well-ordered sentences full of cliches and abstractions, that made himself sound really great and likable. Dave Eggers was confident and strong. He believed in himself. Unlike us who were full of self-doubt and confusion about our identities.

Margo finished her wine. She told us when the magazine would be out and to send our addresses to her email and she would send us free copies. It was believable. Margo was the kind of person that would send free copies.

20.

We went to Popeye's. Popeye's was down the street from Petra's apartment. It was a place where people eat fried chicken. It was like Kentucky Fried Chicken. Why it was not Kentucky Fried Chicken I do not know. It seemed and looked like the same exact place. Why it was called Popeye's I do not know either. I assumed that Popeye ate spinach. There was no spinach there.

John was nervous and got terribly drunk. He kept jumping on Jason and making comments about having sex with me.

We went to Popeye's because Jason needed to digitally video tape a promo for his new book. The eating at Popeye's was supposed to be ironic and iconic and perhaps morbidly depressing.

We went in Popeye's.

All of us walked with drunken swaggers.

The lighting was horrible.

There were scattered people sitting eating. An older Puerto Rican and a white man and woman who looked homeless. Nobody seemed happy to be feasting on fried chicken.

We stood at the counter. John was running around screaming, "FRIED CHICKEN, BITCHES!"

Hu Chin and Petra were both holding cameras getting different angles.

A young Asian man stood at the register. He was over-weight and considered his job as a worker at Popeye's honorable.

I ordered a chicken bowl. Which consisted of corn, fried chicken and mashed potatoes. Everybody else pitched in and bought a 12 piece. The meal was only supposed to be a snack because we were supposed to go to a party at a bar and then go out for a real meal at the end of the night.

John Walters very excitedly said to the Asian man working the register, "Isn't America awesome?"

The man at the register replied, "What would you like to drink?"

John persisted, "America, this is my homeland. I'm from Homeland Security and I want to know if you think America is awesome. If you do not I'll consider you a terrorist and then I'll waterboard your dick off."

The man at the register, "What would you like to drink?"

John Walters said politely, "Hmm, a Mountain Dew. I'm from Philly, I'm ghetto."

The Asian man did not know what the fuck he was talking about.

We all sat down together like a big family of assholes.

Hu Chin and Petra kept recording.

Jason and John ate their chicken like savages from a movie, devouring each piece in the most absurd way. I didn't know what was going on. No one had informed me of the experiment in meat eating. Hu Chin then put the camera down and ate fried chicken. Usually he was a god of Vegan Behavior. He wrote many Blog posts on the evils of meat-eating. His theory was that gazelles run away from lions, therefore we shouldn't eat meat. It was logical. There he was eating chicken. I had assumed that Jason and John were also vegans. Nobody seemed to mention it though. Everyone was happily eating meat. I always ate meat. My father was a meat cutter and he served predominately meat. My family hunted deer and small game. I had never hunted but had killed many animals with a pellet gun when I was little. Everyone was talking about Veganism lately. The killing of animals seemed natural to me. Humans had the power and they killed the animals. The Romans had the power and took over Europe, Europe had the power and took over the Americas. America had the power and took over Iraq and Afghanistan. It all seemed natural to me. I was a novelist, not a political poet or politician, not an activist. Ethics was my least favorite part of philosophy. I enjoyed epistemology.

John Walters finished a fried chicken leg and yelled, "MY FUCKING LEFT NUT IS A RECTANGLE!"

A middle-aged Puerto Rican walked by and John Walters yelled at him, "I'M FUCKING PROTESTANT, DO YOU KNOW WHAT THAT MEANS! I'VE A FINGER AND AN ASSHOLE, DO YOU KNOW WHAT THEY HAVE IN COMMON. I WALK DOGS AND MAKE MORE THAN THE PRESIDENT!"

Petra was taping the whole thing. She was not having a fun time. She wasn't smiling. Her expression was that of a serious person documenting a serious event in literary history.

John Walters said to Hu Chin loudly, "I like summer, Hu. I like when I've been sweating all fucking day. Then I go in the bathroom and put my middle finger between my two balls and rub my finger around on my sweaty genitals."

Petra said from behind the digital camera, "I like when my vagina is sweaty."

Walters said, "I like when your vagina is sweaty too."

Petra zoomed in on Jason and Jason noticed and said, "This is really terrific chicken."

Hu Chin said to me, "How is your bowl?"

"It verges on disgusting, but at the same time, it is still kind of good."

Hu Chin nodded that life was good.

A young Indian couple walked by and John Walters said, "I have an Indian proctologist. One of your people has stuck their finger in my ass."

They didn't look happy about that. But it was New York and things like that were bound to happen so they walked to the counter and ordered like nothing had happened.

John Walters said to Hu Chin and I, "I'm taking meaninglessness to new levels. You two don't know meaninglessness. I'm going to get enlightened in the art of meaningless behavior. I will be the Buddha of meaninglessness." Then he screamed, "I WILL FUCK THE GODS OF TIMES SQUARE WHILE I WALK THEIR DOGS!"

Everyone ate meat and loved it. Everyone looked bad in the lighting. Why they would choose such a bad lighting scheme was beyond me. It accentuated everyone's pock marks and scars and made everyone's skin look horrible.

We finished eating and walked down the street. Hu Chin came up to me and said he felt sick. I said, "That's why I ate that little bowl. I eat meat every day but that shit makes me feel sick."

"I ate a chicken sandwich from McDonald's the other day."

"How did you feel then?"

"Okay."

Before Hu Chin spoke his brain ran a series of sentences through his head. He always picked the shortest sentence possible. He did not engage in monologues or soliloquies. I only spoke in questions or in long monologues, like I was writing an impromptu Blog post.

I said, "Between the alcohol and that shit we just ate we are all going to have rancid farts in about an hour. We are going to be semi-famous writers about to appear in a major magazine farting all over New York City."

Hu Chin laughed.

I asked him, "Are you still doing push-ups?"

"A little."

"I tried to exercise. I stopped smoking for six months this year and ran laps around my block. I did like 50 push-ups a day. Did like 50 crunches. Nothing happened. I did it to impress some girl."

"Was she impressed?"

"I never told her. I felt embarrassed. She went to a gym and had a sweet cell phone. She wants a man who goes to the gym and has a sweet cell phone too with unlimited text messaging."

"It would be funny to be in a gym."

"I can't imagine being in a gym. Everyone in there sweating, wearing funny outfits. I couldn't handle the absurdity of it. I would get an attack of nausea and have to run out."

"The other day I was walking down the street and saw somebody from my college and ran."

"Did they notice you running?"

"No."

"Remember several years ago when we kept writing to each other, 'what are we supposed to do?'"

"Yeah."

"We kept doing things. Nothing happened. Every year I keep getting more and more adjusted to how boring life is."

"The other day I peeled a banana, then ate the banana and felt fine."

"Did you really?"

"Ten minutes later I sat in bed and did nothing for two hours."

21.

The party at the bar was for an Internet literary journal that prints a hard copy version that was famous in the world of Internet literary journals that print hard copy versions. I had never been published at the site. I was rejected once and the editor said my grammar was fucked up. The editor was supposed to be there. His name was Randal Simms. Randal Simms was famous for hosting readings with semi-famous writers and having people like Moby show up. The writers at his readings were all well-trained at MFA schools and had sensibilities. They were the kind of writers that appeared in McSweeney's and collections edited by Dave Eggers. They weren't my kind of writers. They were sitting in their nice apartments or dorm rooms reading the latest Haruki Murakami story while I was sitting in a shitty little ramshackle house reading a used copy of Erskine Caldwell's *God's Little Acre*. They weren't bad people. They all did volunteer work, voted Democrat and believed in the goodness of humanity. I voted Democrat, needed Habitat for Humanity to come to my house and knew from personal experience the shittiness of humanity because I was shitty myself.

We entered the bar. It was full of people wearing nice clothes and drinking peacefully. It was the kind of bar where no one ever got into a fight. I walked through the bar looking for Desmond but he wasn't there. Petra came over with a Captain and Coke and handed it to me. I gulped and felt a little better.

We all sat in the back. There were people everywhere. Horrible techno music was playing. It was awful. Jason sat next to me. Petra walked around talking to everyone, being friendly. She was a good woman. She didn't bother her man or nag or bitch at him to pay attention to her. I could walk around freely and make conversation to people. And she could walk around freely and talk to people. I didn't care if she flirted with men and she didn't care if I flirted with women.

Randal Simms was wearing a white suit and had long emo hair. He looked like a 13 year old boy. He was a very pretty man. In a dress and wig and some estrogen pills he could have pulled off being female. He was very excited to be the host of the party. He ran around talking to everyone making sure everyone knew who he was and that he was the host. Everyone was very impressed. Randal Simms seemed really happy that everyone was impressed. While sitting there a cute woman in her late 20s told me she worked for a magazine. I told her I had several books published. She was impressed. I was impressed with her working for a magazine. Everyone was happy to be impressed.

Jason Bassini was sitting next to me, we spoke to each other yelling because the music was so fucking loud. Jason said, "Everything is hierarchy here. Everyone instantly announces their job, which implies their status and how much money they make. No one does that in Seattle. Everyone just sits around and asks if you want to get stoned."

"This is New York City, this is where you come if you want to achieve status. People go to Seattle to become like musicians or something."

"I don't know why people live in Seattle."

"People in Youngstown sit around all day bitching about their problems."

"People don't do that in Seattle. People are always like, 'Life is awesome, lets go do something. Lets get a haircut.'"

"People are very concerned with their hair in Seattle?"

Jason said, "Yeah, people love their hair. Everyone is very concerned with how their hair looks. Everyone spends hours deliberating with their friends about what style of haircut and hair color they should have. It is like a command room in a World War 2 movie. Everyone is sitting around staring at maps, discussing strategy, what the enemy is doing and then after long conference with friends they decide on a haircut."

"In Youngstown nobody cares about their hair except for black women. Black women enjoy wearing a variety of strange weaves. Men still spike their hair and get it tinted with blond highlights."

"Are you serious?"

"Yes, very serious."

While I was sitting there a giant Scottish man sat next to me. He tapped me on my shoulder and said, "I'm Liam."

I looked at him confused and said, "I'm Benny Baradat."

Liam was a large Scottish man about 6-5 and 220 pounds. His skin was pale and reddish. His hair was short and combed with precision. He had grown up in Scotland and gone to college there. His parents sent him to America for his master's degree in computer science.

Liam said, "I'm Lyndi and Petra's friend."

"Oh, they told me about you."

"Oh, what did they say?"

Lyndi talked about how awesome he was and Petra said he was dumb, so I said, "Oh, they said there was a Scottish guy they hung out with."

"Yeah, that's me. Are you fucking Petra?"

"Am I what?"

"Fucking Petra?"

I did not want to talk to the giant Scottish man. I went to New York City to get my picture taken and be interviewed, not to talk to giant red blotchy Scottish men, I said, "What do you do?"

"I work for Citibank. I'm the president of their IT department." He said it with an extreme sense of pride. Like he had done the right thing in life. He had made the right choices and lived up to his obligations. He said it not knowing that middle-America had lost total respect for anything or anyone involved in the banking industry. The only people who still had respect for such people were silly girls with lawyer dads who got turned on by foreign accents like Lyndi Wood.

"I work at a steak house."

The Scottish man looked at me like I was a fucking dumbass and said, "Lyndi said you got your picture taken for a pretty big magazine."

"Yes, they took my picture."

He moved in close and smiled like we were buddies, like two guys hanging out watching soccer and said, "So tell me the truth, did you fuck Petra?"

"I slept next to her in bed and she held me while I cried and talked about my mother."

The Scottish man said, "Oh, that's strange."

"That's how I roll," I said.

The Scottish man got up and went somewhere else that was not near me.

I looked at Jason and said, "Why the fuck would a European come here? They have national health care and free college and all kinds of good shit."

"I think they come here for our money."

"Our money was loaned, it's leveraged. It isn't real money."

"Nobody cares if the money is real or not. I don't care."

"Neither do I, as long as I'm holding a bunch of twenties and a couple of fifties. I don't care if there is any truth to it. I just wanna spend it." I said, "I had a credit card when I was 20, it was for 7,000 dollars. I don't know why they gave it to me. I think because my parents made a good amount. I spent 5,000 of it in three months. I didn't care. It just felt so good to be buying things. It feels so good to just get things you want."

"Hu is giving me 1,500 for my poetry book."

"That sounds good, what you gonna buy?"

"A new snow board."

"I've never snowboarded. There's nowhere to snowboard for several hundred miles of where I live."

I got up and looked for Desmond again. Still there was no Desmond. Petra walked up to me and said, "Are you having a good time?" I looked at her and thought she was pretty, after I was done thinking about how pretty she was standing there, I said, "The music is really loud and nothing is happening."

She said, "Both of those statements are true."

"There's some giant Scottish man here that keeps asking me if I've fucked you."

"That Scottish bastard."

"I told him we didn't."

"It's none of his business. He's supposed to be fucking Lyndi Wood."

"I don't know. We should go soon. Desmond isn't here. Hu and John and Jason aren't talking. They are all sitting there staring."

"I'll finish my drink and we'll go."

22.

We came out of the club and Hu introduced me to someone he called Brad. He was a medium sized Asian man. He looked strong and jolly. I didn't understand the jolly. He wore glasses and looked like a good guy. I shook his hand and said, "Hello Brad."

He said, "My name isn't Brad."

"Hu says your name is Brad."

"No, it's Andrew."

"No, you're fucking with me. Your name is Brad."

"No, seriously it's not. My name is Andrew."

I looked at Hu and said, "You lied to me. His name is Andrew."

Andrew or Brad said, "Yeah, that's my name."

"I'm very sorry, can you ever forgive me," I said laughing. I was drunk and not taking anything serious.

"Yeah, okay."

Andrew seemed really happy. I was stunned by his smiling. He seemed to be smiling and looked fresh-faced and American. I looked at Hu Chin and thought he looks Asian, all miserable sad and hard working. Andrew looked happy and hard working like a protestant. I wondered if Andrew was a protestant. So I said out loud because I was drunk and didn't care about anything, "Are you a protestant, Andrew?"

Andrew looked at me like I was nuts. I assume he was contemplating how huge of a racist I was or something.

He said, "Yeah so. Asians can't be protestants?"

"I don't know. I guess so."

"I don't go to church or anything, why would you ask that?"

"I don't know, I'm drunk."

He looked at me like I was a huge asshole..

Andrew said to me, "Asians aren't supposed to smile?"

"Asians are usually miserable people, getting up everyday, sticking to their morals and the work."

Hu Chin couldn't stop laughing. He sat on the stoop laughing hysterically.

Andrew told Hu about a restaurant we should go to. Andrew really liked restaurants and literature. Hu told me that one day Andrew would be the next James Wood. He was not the kind of man that sat around depressed or drinking himself into a stupor. He was the kind of person that while reading he would fill a notebook with notes on the text, research things he found in the text, read biographies and had a passion for finding out what the author meant. Andrew had a brain for literary criticism, he was a good dude, and we all had to find our place in the great republic of literature.

John, Jason, Petra and Lyndi Wood joined us outside. John Walters said he had to go. John said in a drunken tired voice, "My girlfriend wants to rub my balls. She likes my balls."

I gave John a hug and he walked down the street in another direction.

Everyone was pretty drunk. We walked around with the snow falling and no one caring about anything. We were looking for an Asian restaurant to eat our final meal together, Jason was leaving on a plane and I was leaving on a bus the next day.

We found an Asian restaurant that was still open. We entered it. They looked pissed because they all wanted to leave and go somewhere else besides work. We fucked up their lives. They sat us down on the second floor. We were loud and acting drunk. I kept screaming at Lyndi Wood, "Look up irony on your phone?"

Lyndi Wood would yell back, "I just did."

Jason would yell, "Do it again!"

I yelled at Petra, "I'm not eating any sea weed, you eat the sea weed."

She yelled at Hu Chin, "Umami."

"What the fuck is that?" Hu Chin said.

"It's a new taste," Petra said.

Lyndi Wood yelled at me, "Irony is a discordance between what is said and what is meant."

"What the fuck is a discordance, a discrepancy?"

"There's dramatic irony, which means that the characters don't get it, but the audience understands it."

Jason yelled, "The audience understands nothing."

Hu Chin yelled at Petra, "I don't believe there is any taste called umami, you're making shit up."

"I'm not making up, I'm serious."

"No, I don't believe you. There's no truth."

Jason yelled, "Did you know in some countries if you let your dick hair grow it is considered ironic?"

Lyndi Wood replied, "That is so interesting."

Hu Chin yelled, "There's bitter, sweet, salty and sour. That's it, that's the truth, those are the tastes."

"No, there's umami. It's a fact. Look it up, Lyndi Wood."

"A woman's pussy juice is salty I believe."

Jason yelled, "Yes, very much, salty pussy."

"Some pussies are bitter with irony," I said.

"Oh yes, the ironic vagina," Jason said.

"Umami is found in aged foods with glutamate or something. It says it is found a lot in Chinese and Japanese cuisine," Lyndi Wood said.

"See, Hu. I was right."

Jason said to me, "But what does a taint smell like?"

"Usually not very good. But I think that is why it is so hot to smell one."

Lyndi Wood yelled, "What is a taint?"

Hu Chin said, "The space between the asshole and dick or vagina."

I said, "Why does that space deserve a name?"

Jason said, "There's nothing there but space."

Petra yelled, "No, that's not the taint."

Hu, "Then what's the taint?"

I said to Jason, "Is there a 'the taint' or should we say 'a taint?'"

Jason said, "The taint. The taint is very important and we should never forget that all taints require a 'the.'"

"True," I said.

Hu Chin yelled at Petra, "The taint is the space between the balls and asshole."

"Do I have the taint?" Petra said.

"Yes, as long as you have a space between your vagina and asshole, you have the taint."

Lyndi Wood while looking at her cell phone said, "Yes, Hu Chin is correct. We all have the taint."

Jason, "Thank god Benny, we have the taint."

"What if an army of the taints took over Seattle?"

"I would give up peacefully and believe in their God."

Petra said, "I still don't understand what the taint is. It isn't anything but space. Why does it need a name?"

Lyndi Wood said, "The Scottish guy just sent me a text message saying he might want to fuck me later this week."

Hu Chin said, "Umami is stupid."

Jason said, "Is it Scots or Irish who wear kilts?"

I said, "It doesn't matter, seriously."

Jason said, "You mean like the fact at all."

"No, that fact doesn't matter."

Petra yelled, "Hu, you don't know anything about taste."

Hu replied, "Is that a question?"

"No, it's a declarative sentence."

"I have two small dogs, one day I will order them to eat you, Petra," Hu said.

"I bet you fucking will, Hu Chin," said Petra.

"No doubt, Petra," Hu yelled.

"The Scottish wrote me another text message. It is really sweet," Lyndi Wood said.

"Irony is when your ass tells your face that there is love in the universe," I said.

Jason yelled at me, "What if my dick had discordance with my balls?"

"Is that a thought experiment?" I said.

"Yes, very deep and incomprehensible," Jason said.

"Nothing matters except irony. I have trained myself in the mixed martial arts of irony. I am now I'm an irony sensei. I conquer towns and cities with irony," Hu Chin said in an ancient voice.

"You're not Japanese, Hu," said Petra.

"Someday my dogs will kill you, Petra."

"I am stronger than your dogs."

"My dogs are a mighty force," Hu Chin said in a serious tone of voice.

"This is really interminable," Jason said to me.

"No, this is the apex of human experience," I said.

"I don't believe you," said Jason.

"No, this is like the meaning of life. The meaning of all things, logos, the principle that guides the universe," I said.

"This can't mean anything," said Jason.

Lyndi Wood yelled, "The Scottish guy wants to see me tomorrow night for drinks."

Petra said, "Didn't you already see each other for drinks tonight?"

"Everybody is getting drinks," I said.

"If everybody is getting drinks, then nobody is getting drinks," said Jason.

"Bean curd is fucking awesome," said Hu Chin.

"Hmm, you're right. I might start eating this more often," I said.

"I'm fucking Asian and I can't pick this tofu up with chopsticks," said Petra.

"They should send you back to Tennessee for such dishonorable behavior," I said.

"Why don't you go somewhere and feel guilty, you Christian bastard."

"The Catholic God is the only God for me," said Jason.

Hu Chin said in a serious tone of voice, "I don't understand, who is God, God or Jesus?"

Jason said, "They are both God."

"In the beginning there was the Word, and the Word was with God, and the Word was God," I said.

Petra said, "You know that doesn't help anything at all. That sounded like a lot of fucking gibberish."

Jason said, "You're all going to hell."

"The God of The Taint," Hu Chin said.

"The Scottish guy text messaged me again," Lyndi Wood said smiling.

23.

The party was all over. I was back in Petra's bed naked. We had sex and were laying there. It was dark in the room. No music was playing. We weren't smoking. It was a no smoking apartment. I didn't have an orgasm which frustrated her. But she was fine with it. She didn't have one either. We were people that didn't have orgasms. Orgasms don't matter that much when you have a nice lower east side apartment.

Petra said, "We look good walking around together."

I was puzzled by what she said and replied, "That never occurred to me."

"I think people see us and think we look good together, like a good artsy New Yorker couple."

"It never occurred to me that people were looking at us."

"People are looking at us all the time."

"Are you sure?"

"Oh yeah, that's what New York is about. It is about looking good in front of other people," Petra said.

"I don't know. I'm not concerned."

"If you wanna be a big shot writer you better get concerned."

"Well, if you think we looked good. I believe your opinion."

"My opinion is correct."

"I think this whole us meeting each other thing turned out okay."

"Yeah, it did. I didn't know what you would be like. There was this one guy who came to visit me when I lived in Austin. He bought me dinner and took me out. When we came back to my place he went in the bedroom took off all his clothes and laid on my bed. I went in the bedroom and he was there totally naked. We hadn't even kissed. I got really mad. I didn't tell him I was mad though. I stood there and explained in the most polite voice possible how I thought we were just friends and it was so 1955 that he thought I would just have sex with him because he bought me things. And that it was 2008 and men and women could be friends now. He didn't seem happy about that all. He put his clothes back on and went to the couch. I took a Vicodin I had and went to sleep."

"You're silly."

"Yeah, that was pretty silly."

"Tomorrow I leave," I said.

"I know, I'm sad. It will be all over. I think I'm falling in love with you."

"Is that true?"

"Yeah, I don't know why. I think we get along good. We've talked for almost two years online and we're still sitting here talking. If our relationship was just going to be fucking, you would have given up by now."

"Why would I have given up?"

"Boys who just want to fuck girls will only try for a certain amount of time, like six months or so. But this has been several years."

"Yeah, you remind me of my mother."

"Is that a good or bad thing?" said Petra.

"Well, you both talk a lot and are really erratic and manipulative. But you don't have the whole racist republican thing."

"You think I'm manipulative?"

"Yeah, but I find that endearing."

"Not many people do."

"That's because you probably just manipulated them."

"I don't manipulate you."

"Only when I want you too," I said.

"Then that means you manipulated me."

"Yes, but you don't know I've manipulated you. You still assume you have done the manipulation."

"I enjoy this game."

"It's the only game worth playing," I said.

"Having a dick in my mouth makes the world go away."

24.

The next and last day of the New York City trip nothing special was supposed to happen. I was supposed to live through the day and around 9 I would get on the bus and go back to Ohio. The only exciting thing that was going to happen was Petra's friend Sonia was coming to visit for a couple of days and we were supposed to go to a Christmas Party at Melville House in Dumbo. All Petra did was have people visit. I'm not sure if she did anything but have people visit and get drunk. It seemed like a good life. Live in a nice little apartment on the lower east of Manhattan, get drunk at night with friends, hang out, do dumb shit, talk dumb shit, never discuss anything serious. Then get up, eat a nice breakfast. Maybe go to the post office, go to a bakery, get a man to buy lunch and a drink at a nice bar. Read a book, buy some books, admire New York City, feel good about the choices you've made in life. Check Craiglist for jobs, get drunk again. Get a man to buy you a nice dinner. Walk down the street admiring New York City, text message someone. Text message someone else. Admire New York City. Have a celebrity spotting. Get drunk with friends.

It was a really good life Petra led. She was happy. This is what the liberal and the republican media told people to do, they told us to make ourselves happy. They said, "People, make yourselves happy. Because there is no God." People always thought if no one believed in God and we were nihilists then people would go around murdering each other. That didn't happen at all, we just bought a lot of things with credit.

Sonia was a half-Mexican half-white American from Texas. She grew up in a good neighborhood. She didn't grow up in poverty speaking Spanish riding on buses and sweating without air-conditioning down in Texas. No, she had it okay. She was from the middle-class. She didn't have a dad, only a mom. Her dad was somewhere. She didn't know where. He had left so long ago she didn't even care. The only thing that remained was a ghostlike abandonment issue that haunted her romantic life. She didn't care for romance though: she went to an expensive college. Sonia was in her senior year. Her loans added up to over 100,000 dollars. She planned on going to law school and making her loans total 2 maybe 300,000 dollars. She was convinced she would be a wealthy lawyer. She had gone to good schools and shown proficiency, there was going to be no stopping her. She had perfect grades, even in modern biology. She was a memorization machine. You gave her sentences and titles, she memorized them. She was a master at sudoku which led to getting a 162 on the LSAT. The sky was the limit, she was the future of the American legal profession.

I was sitting in the kitchen on a stool drinking coffee when Sonia came in. Sonia was pretty, nice little cheeks, beautiful curly hair, not the most attractive, but in terms of women who become lawyers she was hot. She was going to be a hot lawyer.

When she came in Petra ran over. They hugged each other and jumped up and down and made a lot of noise. This is how women who haven't seen each other in a long time greet each other in America. No matter where you fucking are. They run over, hug, jump up and down twice, sometimes three times. And during all that movement and action they are making a lot of fucking noise.

Petra introduced Sonia to me. We shook hands. I didn't care about meeting Sonia. The trip was almost over. I had met enough people. She wasn't a writer. She was going to be a lawyer. I was tired and needed rest, not another person acting out in my presence. Petra and Sonia sat in the bedroom talking about trivial shit that didn't matter. Petra was showing Sonia her new dresses. Sonia was trying them on. Sonia was walking around in her underwear. Then Petra suggested that I strip down to my blue long underwear and black socks and Sonia stay in her underwear and we take pictures wearing funny hats in the kitchen.

I had never played fake model before. I had always seen fellow writers and fans' Photo Buckets and Facebooks full of 1000s of pictures of themselves playing fake model. Them standing there looking "real" or "emotional" or "attractive," posing for the camera. I never understood it. The only time I thought pictures should be taken is when you are on vacation, you stand in front of The Grand Canyon with your brother or girlfriend and take a picture. There is no other reason to take a picture. But everyone in New York was very adamant about pictures. It was important to have one's image recorded as many times as possible for the sake of what, I don't know, ask a sociology professor.

Best Behavior

I participated in their event without complaining. Sonia and I posed together in like 30 different positions. I noticed that Sonia had a lot of sweet tattoos. She was the tattooed lawyer. I got the urge to have sex with Sonia. But then I felt greedy and decided not to care about Sonia. Petra was very happy taking the pictures. She was showing how artsy she was to me. Sonia was showing how sexy she was. It was all really pagan. After the pictures were taken. We sat and looked at them. They all looked like two people standing there. I had no shirt on and a very serious expression on my face. I wondered why. I knew then I was playing model too. It was fun to pretend you were sexy for a little bit. There was no truth to it. I knew I was not sexy. There was nothing sexy about me. I was not cool. It was okay, I had learned to deal with it. The pictures were dumb. Then Sonia took pictures of Petra and I on the bed looking cute together, like a couple, like we were "in love." We weren't in love, we weren't in lust, we weren't in anything. We weren't two lonely people meeting in the night either. There was nothing awesome or amazing about our relationship. It was just another dumb slogan in New York City. Benny Baradat Dates Petra for $25.99 get 10% off on Tuesdays. Everything was a slogan in New York City, everything was publicity. She was publicity, I was publicity, our clothes, our eyes, everything a slogan to sell more units or to get into better parties. There was nothing inherently wrong with the relationship. We weren't evil people, we didn't beat each other, I didn't get Petra pregnant and abandon the kid and not pay child support. We merely considered our relationship a slogan, a flashy commercial, I'm not even sure if it was supposed to be a real life experience.

Petra and I pretended we were in love on the bed. Cuddling, looking warmly into each other's eyes, at one point I grabbed her breast and laughed, everybody laughed and felt very happy. It was completely predictable: the boy always does something stupid and the girls laugh and everyone pretends it's spontaneous. New York City was starting to get to me. There was too much paganism for me. There was too much nihilism and pointlessness. There was nihilism back in Youngstown, but not like in New York. I couldn't wait for the bus to come.

The girls tried to convince me to call off work and go home with Sonia who was traveling down I-80 the next day. I called people at work, pretending I wanted to stay another day. I wanted to stay another day to have sex again. I realized that and felt stupid. Petra and Sonia kept yelling at me to stay another day. They told me not to show up for work, they would forgive me, it was just a steak house, who cares. That infuriated me, but I didn't tell them that. They considered my job, what I did to feed myself and pay bills a joke. If I stayed there I would just be this nice little blue collar boy to play with. I really felt demoralized being there. I didn't mention it though: it didn't seem like their business. They had their own version of reality, their own version of how life should be lived, and I wasn't going to change that. I was surrounded by Petra, Sonia and Lyndi Wood was down the hall, three women that were completely accustomed to getting what they wanted. I was from a world where one did not get what they wanted, and was happy if they got anything at all. There was a huge discrepancy in our world views.

Petra took a shower. Sonia and I were left alone in the kitchen drinking coffee. Sonia was eating seaweed and rice. She looked happy chewing on the seaweed. There were no pictures anymore. Just two people standing there waiting for time to pass. So I said, "You gonna be a lawyer?"

"Yeah," Sonia said.

"What you think of the election?"

"I voted for Obama, but I think a lot of people are going to be disappointed when he doesn't deliver all the things he promised."

The answer was a cliché and I could tell she had said it a thousand times.

"Do you think people will really care if he delivers or not?"

She looked at me funny and said, "I don't know."

I sat there thinking, while she ate seaweed, writers are all terrible Hobbesians. You can do Lockean things with people, give them money, incentives, benefits, trophies, but that isn't anything but putting cheese in front of mice. Their real nature was Hobbesian. They all want to be told what to do, they all need outside motivation (cheese), they don't care about political issues, all they care about is blow jobs, pot smoking, stupid trivial shit. Most of them don't even know where roads and electricity come from. As soon as chaos breaks loose they start killing each other. As long as Obama maintains the roads and keeps everything in line they'll vote for him again. If he does great things then that's an added bonus. People voted for Bush again even though Bush did nothing his first four years but fuck things up. Writers believe in Plato's *guardians*, Dostoevsky's *keepers of the mystery* because normal everyday people have no clue what is going on, and will never know. As long as they are well fed and have shelter they don't care if something bad is happening or if something good is happening. If things get bad enough, but what is bad enough? Reagan and Clinton were voted back in, both of the administrations were nothing but decadence overload. King Louis the 14th built Versailles, led a great empire, two generations later his grandkid is getting his head cut off by the peasants. Houellebecq said in a book that we need to invent new humans, if we had better improved humans then things would turn out better. Better than what? Humans do not want to be better. A person may want to swim better or have a better smile. But they don't want humanity to swim better or have a better smile. It isn't even a question of "want," they don't care. I don't care. Nobody really cares about people in Uganda or wherever people are blowing each other's brains out. People aren't designed to care about shit that happens thousands of miles away or to people not in their tribe. Humans lived in tribes and small villages for 100,000 years before they ever built the first cities. In those early cities each person was assigned a little task to do, like stone mason, farmer, or carpenter and lived out those tasks until they died at thirty. As Plato said they were supposed to mind their own business while doing it. I think the problem industrialization has caused is that it requires a very awesome species. A species that can care about shit on a large scale. Not a species that concerns itself with the whitening of their teeth and what kind of cell phone they have. Most humans consider senior prom the apex of their life on this planet anyway.

25.

Night came early. The solstice was two weeks away. Petra, Lyndi Wood and Sonia and I were walking down the streets of Dumbo looking for the Melville House Christmas Party. Everybody was supposed to be there; Hu Chin, John Walters, and Tom White were going to meet us there. Then after, Tom was going to escort me to the bus station.

Dumbo was a strange place. All the buildings were big and wide, but not high. There was a lot of girth in the district. As we walked down the street the women kept talking. I didn't know what they talking about. It didn't excite me at all.

We found the building. We went in. It was magical. It was like being in City Lights or Shakespeare and Company. Oh, not really. But it was close. I pretended. I used my imagination. Dennis Loy Johnson walked up to me and shook my hand. I said, "I'm Benny Baradat."

He said, "I'm Dennis Johnson."

He forgot the "Loy," but I forgave him.

We talked for a moment about trivial shit. He seemed really nice. I mentioned that I listened to his podcast several times and enjoyed it. He said he read a couple things I wrote and enjoyed them. We kissed each other's ass, it was good. It was going to be a good party of people being nice to each other. It was Christmas and baby Jesus may even love writers and publishers.

I didn't mention to Dennis Johnson that he had rejected a crappy short book I wrote. It was not a good book, I had admitted to myself on several occasions. I was okay with him not publishing it. So I didn't bring it up.

There was beer and wine and chips. There was no bathroom. I walked everywhere and could not find a place to shit. I could feel pressure on my rectum. There was a nice white collar woman who gave me a key and told me directions to get to the bathroom, which was outside. I went outside and walked down the sidewalk. It was cold and dark outside. I was alone. Felt like I was in a horror movie trying to find a door to get away from a space alien.

Found the door and went in. It led to anther door and then to another door. Finally found a place to shit. It was cold in the bathroom. Everything was blue, gray and sad. It was the first time in a while I was alone in several days. I shit slowly not trying to rush anything because it felt so good to be alone again.

When I got back to the party, Hu Chin was there. He had a strange young man with him wearing what looked like train conductor overalls and a nice white shirt under them. His hair was brown and soft looking, well combed and conditioned and his eyes stared nowhere in particular. I looked at Hu and said, "Who's this guy?"

"That's Ronald."

Ronald came over and shook my hand and said, "I'm an artist."

I replied, "That's good."

Ronald sat down and drew a picture of a hamster being eaten by a single Nike shoe.

Tom White showed up. I was very excited to see him. He was my anchor in New York. He was the only person I knew there that had a sense of rationality and responsibility. I went over to Tom White, I said, "This place is full of sin."

He said, "Do you want me to bring you to the local Catholic Church to get the Eucharist?"

"No, not like that. Not religious. Maybe religious. I don't know. It isn't spiritual. Everyone is just drinking, having a good time."

"Isn't that what's life about? You're supposed to have a good time."

"I don't know. That is like television philosophy or something. I don't know, I somehow missed that part of American socialization."

"I just go to work and pay my bills. I have access to things like the opera and they show Fassbinder movies in the theaters here. I enjoy that. It isn't all sin."

"What did you do when you first got here?"

He had a look of remembering and said, "Got drunk a lot and went to parties."

"See, sin."

"There's something very Catholic about you."

I stood there. Looked around the room. Everyone seemed okay. No one was happy, no one was miserable. It was cold outside and they were at a party. Maybe it wasn't so bad. Petra, Lyndi Wood and Sonia were standing by the chips. They were talking, smiling, having a pleasant time. Everything was pleasant. And if it wasn't they could always drink more alcohol.

At one point Lin came in. The woman I had spent time with last summer in New York. She looked cute. I wanted to talk to her. She walked around, spoke to people, but not to me. I wanted to kiss her and tell her something like I loved her, or would love her forever, or that she needed to have my baby. Which were all lies. But it would have been fun to lie. I saw people have fun lying all the time, why couldn't I? I didn't tell her anything though. Went over to Hu Chin and said, "Tell Lin it is okay to talk to me. I want to talk to her."

Hu Chin went over to her. She was crying. Hu Chin was surprised. Hu Chin didn't act surprised, he maintained a neutral facial expression. Lin said, "I gotta go." Lin didn't specify it was because of me, because she was a tough person. And tough people don't specify names in public.

Lin walked out the door. I went to the door and stood outside, it was cold. She was already down the street. I saw her walking down the sidewalk toward the subway, she was going to ride the subway alone, being sad, wishing she had never taken the subway to the stupid Melville House Christmas Party. Dennis Loy Johnson was standing next to the chips holding a glass of wine not knowing that his Christmas Party celebrating the birth of baby Jesus caused a young woman to cry. I yelled out for Lin, I yelled her name, "LIN!" She didn't respond. I don't know if she couldn't hear me or she didn't want to give a shit about me. I watched her turn right behind a building. Petra was inside convinced I was "in love" with her. I was outside pining over a woman named Lin who told me once in a bar while we were drinking mixed drinks that she loved *Growth of the Soil* by Knut Hamsun. Lin was gone: down a sidewalk onto a subway onto another sidewalk into her bed away from me. There was no commitment here. No long enduring anything. Everything happened on a Saturday and was turned into ashes by Tuesday.

Went back in to the party. Everyone was talking. What they were talking about, I don't know. I don't think it was books. I'm not even sure how to talk about books. Usually everyone just supplies a list of the last couple of books they read, says "wonderful" or "slow" and then the conversation ends.

Tom White and I put on our coats. Petra came over, she looked sad. Her face looked not so happy. I had a sad look on my face also. We both had sad looks on our faces like two people who had been having a good time and fucking for two days should have when parting from each other. We went outside in the cold, with snow fluttering down around us, landing on our coats and hair. Tom White walked ahead to give us personal space. Petra said, "I don't want you to go."

I said, "I have to."

We kissed. It was not a crazy mad passionate kiss. It was soft and polite, a respectable kiss. Petra started crying. I saw tears come from her eyes. I enjoyed the idea of a woman crying for me. She enjoyed having a reason to cry. We were both having a good time. We hugged one last time. And we walked in two different directions.

I caught up to Tom White and we made our way back to Manhattan. Tom said, "That looked pretty dramatic. You all right?"

"I guess. I mean, what else is to be done. I have to get on a bus. That's my fate."

Tom didn't say anything. He gave me a minute to realign my senses and focus on what needed to be done. Tom and I needed to have a really good conversation before I left. I needed to give my confession before I got on the bus. Tom knew that. Tom knew he had been the one that talked before and now it was my turn.

We made it to the subway and I still hadn't talked. There was silence. Two men walking in silence together. We rode the subway in silence. As we walked up the stairs to Times Square I said, "There is no enlightenment."

Tom knew I had begun. I continued, "There is no enlightenment..... I don't feel good at all..... I'm detached, I have no consideration for the results..... I am disciplined..... But still nothing..... The only thing that cheers me up is mint chocolate chip ice cream and horror movies..... A long list of predicates culminating - Real boredom.... Real boredom.... Real boredom.... Real boredom..... Real boredom.... Real boredom..... Real boredom..... Real boredom.... Real boredom.... Real boredom.... Real boredom.... Real boredom.... Real boredom.... Real boredom.... Real boredom.... Real boredom..... Real boredom.... Real boredom..... Real boredom..... Real boredom.... Real boredom.... Real boredom.... Real boredom.... Real boredom.... Real boredom.... Real boredom.... Real boredom.... Real boredom..... Real boredom.... Real boredom..... Real boredom..... Real boredom.... Real boredom.... Real boredom.... Real boredom.... Real boredom.... Real boredom.... Real boredom.... Real boredom.... Real boredom..... Real boredom.... Real boredom..... Real boredom..... Real boredom.... Real boredom.... Real boredom.... Real boredom.... Real boredom..... Real boredom.... Real boredom..... Real boredom..... Real boredom.... Real boredom.... Real boredom.... Real boredom.... Real boredom.... Real boredom.... Real boredom.... Real boredom.... Real boredom..... Real boredom.... Real boredom..... Real boredom..... Real

boredom.... Real boredom.... Real boredom.... Real boredom.... Real
boredom.... Real boredom.... Real boredom.... Real boredom.... Real
boredom..... Real boredom.... Real boredom..... Real boredom..... Real
boredom.... Real boredom.... Real boredom.... Real boredom.... Real
boredom.... Real boredom.... Real boredom.... Real boredom.... Real
boredom..... Real boredom.... Real boredom..... Real boredom..... Real
boredom.... Real boredom.... Real boredom.... Real boredom.... Real
boredom.... Real boredom.... Real boredom.... Real boredom.... Real
boredom..... Real boredom.... Real boredom..... Real boredom..... Real
boredom.... Real boredom.... Real boredom.... Real boredom.... Real
boredom.... Real boredom.... Real boredom.... Real boredom.... Real
boredom..... Real boredom.... Real boredom..... Real boredom..... Real
boredom.... Real boredom.... Real boredom.... Real boredom.... Real
boredom.... Real boredom.... Real boredom.... Real boredom.... Real
boredom..... Real boredom.... Real boredom..... Real boredom..... Real
boredom.... Real boredom.... Real boredom.... Real boredom.... Real
boredom.... Real boredom.... Real boredom.... Real boredom.... Real
boredom..... Real boredom.... Real boredom..... Real boredom..... Real
boredom.... Real boredom.... Real boredom.... Real boredom.... Real
boredom.... Real boredom.... Real boredom.... Real boredom.... Real
boredom..... Real boredom.... Real boredom..... Real boredom..... Real
boredom.... Real boredom.... Real boredom.... Real boredom.... Real
boredom.... Real boredom.... Real boredom.... Real boredom.... Real
boredom..... Real boredom.... Real boredom..... Real boredom..... Real
boredom.... Real boredom.... Real boredom.... Real boredom.... Real
boredom.... Real boredom.... Real boredom.... Real boredom.... Real
boredom..... Real boredom.... Real boredom..... Real boredom..... Real
boredom.... Real boredom.... Real boredom.... Real boredom.... Real
boredom.... Real boredom.... Real boredom.... Real boredom.... Real
boredom..... Real boredom.... Real boredom..... Real boredom..... Real
boredom.... Real boredom.... Real boredom.... Real boredom.... Real
boredom.... Real boredom.... Real boredom.... Real boredom.... Real
boredom..... Real boredom.... Real boredom..... Real boredom..... Real
boredom.... Real boredom.... Real boredom.... Real boredom.... Real
boredom.... Real boredom.... Real boredom.... Real boredom.... Real
boredom..... Real boredom.... Real boredom..... Real boredom..... Real
boredom.... Real boredom.... Real boredom.... Real boredom.... Real
boredom.... Real boredom.... Real boredom.... Real boredom.... Real

boredom..... Real boredom.... Real boredom..... Real boredom..... Real
boredom.... Real boredom.... Real boredom.... Real boredom.... Real
boredom.... Real boredom.... Real boredom.... Real boredom.... Real
boredom..... Real boredom.... Real boredom..... Real boredom..... Real
boredom.... Real boredom.... Real boredom.... Real boredom.... Real
boredom.... Real boredom.... Real boredom.... Real boredom.... Real
boredom..... Real boredom.... Real boredom..... Real boredom..... Real
boredom.... Real boredom.... Real boredom.... Real boredom.... Real
boredom.... Real boredom.... Real boredom.... Real boredom.... Real
boredom..... Real boredom.... Real boredom..... Real boredom..... Real
boredom.... Real boredom.... Real boredom.... Real boredom.... Real
boredom.... Real boredom.... Real boredom.... Real boredom.... Real
boredom..... Real boredom.... Real boredom..... Real boredom..... Real
boredom.... Real boredom.... Real boredom.... Real boredom.... Real
boredom.... Real boredom.... Real boredom.... Real boredom.... Real
boredom..... Real boredom.... Real boredom..... Real boredom..... Real
boredom.... Real boredom.... Real boredom.... Real boredom.... Real
boredom.... Real boredom.... Real boredom.... Real boredom.... Real
boredom..... Real boredom.... Real boredom..... Real boredom..... Real
boredom.... Real boredom.... Real boredom.... Real boredom.... Real
boredom.... Real boredom.... Real boredom.... Real boredom.... Real
boredom..... Real boredom.... Real boredom..... Real boredom..... Real
boredom.... Real boredom.... Real boredom.... Real boredom.... Real
boredom.... Real boredom.... Real boredom.... Real boredom.... Real
boredom..... Real boredom.... Real boredom..... Real boredom..... Real
boredom.... Real boredom.... Real boredom.... Real boredom.... Real
boredom.... Real boredom.... Real boredom.... Real boredom.... Real
boredom..... Real boredom.... Real boredom..... Real boredom..... Real
boredom.... Real boredom.... Real boredom.... Real boredom.... Real
boredom.... Real boredom.... Real boredom.... Real boredom.... Real
boredom..... Real boredom.... Real boredom..... Real boredom..... Real
boredom.... Real boredom.... Real boredom.... Real boredom.... Real
boredom.... Real boredom.... Real boredom.... Real boredom.... Real
boredom..... Real boredom.... Real boredom..... Real boredom..... Real
boredom.... Real boredom.... Real boredom.... Real boredom.... Real

boredom.... Real boredom.... Real boredom.... Real boredom.... Real
boredom..... Real boredom.... Real boredom..... Real boredom..... Real
boredom.... Real boredom.... Real boredom.... Real boredom.... Real
boredom.... Real boredom.... Real boredom.... Real boredom.... Real
boredom..... Real boredom.... Real boredom..... Real boredom..... Real
boredom.... Real boredom.... Real boredom.... Real boredom.... Real
boredom.... Real boredom.... Real boredom.... Real boredom.... Real
boredom..... Real boredom.... Real boredom..... Real boredom..... Real
boredom.... Real boredom.... Real boredom.... Real boredom.... Real
boredom.... Real boredom.... Real boredom.... Real boredom.... Real
boredom..... Real boredom.... Real boredom..... Real boredom..... Real
boredom.... Real boredom.... Real boredom.... Real boredom.... Real
boredom.... Real boredom.... Real boredom.... Real boredom.... Real
boredom..... Real boredom.... Real boredom..... Real boredom..... Real
boredom.... Real boredom.... Real boredom.... Real boredom.... Real
boredom.... Real boredom.... Real boredom.... Real boredom.... Real
boredom..... Real boredom.... Real boredom..... Real boredom..... Real
boredom.... Real boredom.... Real boredom.... Real boredom.... Real
boredom.... Real boredom.... Real boredom.... Real boredom.... Real
boredom..... Real boredom.... Real boredom..... Real boredom..... Real
boredom.... Real boredom.... Real boredom.... Real boredom.... Real
boredom.... Real boredom.... Real boredom.... Real boredom.... Real
boredom..... Real boredom.... Real boredom..... Real boredom..... Real
boredom.... Real boredom.... Real boredom.... Real boredom.... Real
boredom.... Real boredom.... Real boredom.... Real boredom.... Real
boredom..... Real boredom.... Real boredom..... Real boredom..... Real
boredom.... Real boredom.... Real boredom.... Real boredom.... Real
boredom....

FOOTNOTE

Chapters 12, 13, 14, and 15 of Thomas Hobbes' *Leviathan*: The book was given to me by Sam Pink, a writer from Chicago. Sam Pink lives in a small apartment with his brother and currently has a mohawk. Sam Pink gave me the book because I sent him a copy of *The Human War* and *Treatise*.

The Second Treatise of Government of John Locke: I got the copy at a thrift store in 2002 in Eugene, Oregon. Eugene, Oregon is a really great place. There are redwoods and hippies everywhere. There is an excess of jam band music. No jam band music was used in the making of this novel.

The Social Contract and *The Origin of Inequality* contained in the same book of Jean-Jacques Rousseau: I got the book at a thrift store in Youngstown called Dorian Books. Dorian Books is really cool. The owner is named Jack. He sits with his cat all day waiting for customers to come in. Usually I'm the only one in there. The cat walks around and minds its own business.

A Theory of Justice and *Political Liberalism* by John Rawls: Sometimes I daydream about writing a gospel of John Rawls. In the gospel there would be a guy with long hair and a beard. He would go around ghettos, gated communities, urban areas like Times Square, Bedford Street, Brooklyn, cornfields, rice patties, oil fields proclaiming The Original Position. He would go up to small children and teach them the ways of The Original Position. Children would kiss his cheek in love. Women would want to have his babies. It would be a good gospel.

What is Metaphysics by Martin Heidegger: My mother gave me this book for Christmas when I was 16. She said, "Noah, you're a man now. You have pubic hair and you can get boners. You need to learn about life, women, and cars. Here is a copy of *What is Metaphysics* by Martin Heidegger." My brothers and dad clapped and told me they loved me. I told my mother, "I love you mom." My mother smiled, my dad smiled, my brothers smiled. Everyone smiled because it was Christmas morning.

The United States Constitution: I got that book as soon as I was born. I was within the border of America, it was my fate. I came out of my mother's vagina and someone came in the room wearing a military uniform, pointed a gun at my head, and then threw the The U.S. Constitution at me. I took it and said, "Goo, goo, gaa, gaa." My mother smiled, talked about Isiah Berlin for awhile and said, "This baby will grow up to be a terrible jackass." Everyone in the room laughed because they had contracted together to spend the next 18 years raising a jackass instead of an emotional stable well-balanced well-ordered high functioning individual.

Epilogue

June 5, 2009.

Six months and two weeks after.

Unemployment risen to 9.4 percent.

Barack Obama, the president.

Objective of visit, watch auditions for making of a movie based off of first book.

Enter Petra's apartment. She doesn't look good. She has a giant zit on her nose. I lost my job at the steak house. Work at Red Lobster. Work like 15 hours a week. There are no hours at work. No one is getting many hours.

Petra has no job.

She had a job making 40,000 a year:

But lost it.

She fucked up the accounting.

Petra and I walk down Bedford. There is something wrong with her face. It looks disfigured. She is sad. Her New York dream is coming apart. Read on Hipster Runoff that many New York dreams are coming apart.

Petra was running out of money.

Went to a store and I bought Captain Morgan's Spiced Rum. She was happy. She didn't pay for anything.

We walked down Bedford in Brooklyn. Hipsters everywhere. Everyone dressed in Urban Outfitters, American Apparel and clothes they bought from vintage sites Online.

Wearing khaki shorts and Scarface t-shirt. I didn't look hip. Petra kept bitching about the hipsters even though she was dressed exactly like them, shopped at the same places and did nothing but be a hipster.

We stopped at a truck, several nice Latinos sold us burritos and tacos after we paid them. Petra didn't pay for anything.

We went back to her place. We stood in her kitchen and ate. There was no kitchen table. Petra poured the rum in to a cup. She drank the rum without ice cubes or mixing it with any other substance. I put Diet Pepsi in with the rum and ice cubes. We ate the Mexican food.

We went up on her roof and smoked cigarettes. She kept bitching that she wanted to come to the movie auditions the next day. I told her no. I told her it was like work. The movie people had paid me money, I had signed contracts. We had contractual agreements. I had maintain a sense of professionalism. She kept bitching. Then talked about how she went to a lot of parties. It was obvious she was drinking a lot. That she was a person that drank everyday and had severe emotional problems.

We went back to her room. I didn't care about having sex. We kissed. She kept drinking the rum. She told me she was on her period. Told her I didn't mind. Told her I came for the movie. Was hoping she would be my friend and we could have fun. That made her mad. She assumed that I only came there for her. Petra drank one glass after another. I was sipping the rum. Petra gave me a blow job. It wasn't remarkable. It was boring. Just in and out. I could give a much better blowjob. Cummed in her mouth. Laid down.

Told her I had been in a car for the last eight hours and needed to go to sleep. Tried to cuddle her. She got mad. Grabbed my penis and started yelling that I should have sex with her. She tugged on my flaccid penis hard. Turned around and scootched across the bed from her. Decided to wake up early and leave before she woke up.

Woke up to Petra crawling over me. She came back to bed, went back to sleep. Got out of the bed and took a shower. Put my clothes on. Put everything in my book bag. Looked at the rum bottle, the rum was gone. Left the room. Occurred to me that I never even looked at her before I left. Didn't even kiss her goodbye. Didn't matter. She was nuts. I was nuts, but not nuts in a mean way.

The sun was up. Barely anyone was on the streets. Took the L to Manhattan. Looked at cell phone, 6:45 a.m. Didn't have to be to the auditions till 11:30 a.m.. Looked at scribbled note in pocket to see where auditions were, decided to walk there. It said, "133 street, 27." It didn't make sense. Wrote the directions down while drinking rum and while Petra wouldn't' shut up. Decided to walk to 133. Started walking. It got hotter and hotter. Walked up Amsterdam, saw many Jews. Saw many signs telling me to watch television shows. Saw many storefronts selling things that bored me. Kept going into Starbucks, taking a shit and buying a coffee. There was a Starbucks everywhere. There were also many McDonald's. I felt good. Needed time to think. Made it to Harlem. Called the movie people, Jack Lemark and Navid. Jack answered, told me I should be on 27th. Told me to get out of Harlem, get on subway. I looked around, only white man for miles. Didn't care. I voted for Barack Obama. I would tell them that and we would be brothers. Found subway on Saint Nicholas. Took subway down. Found auditions.

Went up elevator. Covered in sweat. Knew I was not looking good. Got out of elevator. Walked into production offices or something. Very weird, movie posters and computers everywhere. Actors sitting and walking around, all talking to themselves. There were like eight people saying lines that I wrote seven years before out loud. It was very weird. Felt weirded out.

Navid led me into a small office. It was stuffy in the office. I thought there would be food. I was hungry. Somebody handed me a bagel. Ate the bagel slowly. Drank coffee even though very hot inside office. Actors came in and acted out parts. A skinny man video taped them. Jack Lemark made comments, telling them to try things in a different way. Navid told them to do things he thought would work better. They would ask me to give an opinion. I gave a sociological opinion, everyone looked at me funny but at the same time took me serious. Ate another bagel.

Left the auditions with Navid and Jack Lemark. We went to Grand Central Station. They bought me a ticket to go home in two days. We sat and ate. They talked about money. How much they could get, what actors they could get, how much money each actor could bring in. I sat there eating french fries text messaging Hu Chin. Hu Chin was at the NYU library facing Washington Square Park. He was my only hope to have a place to sleep. There were other places to sleep. But Hu Chin lived with John Walters and I knew we would have a good time together.

Navid and Jack Lamark got on the Q and went to a barbecue. Walked down to Washington Square Park. Badly needed a shower. Was very hot. No wind in Manhattan, all heat in the summer. Remembered *Seven Year Itch*, remembered how they said it got fucking hot in NYC in the summer. They weren't fucking lying. Found Washington Square Park. Sat down on benches in front of library in the shade. An older Black man played jazz to a middle-aged Puerto Rican woman. Hu Chin came out of NYU. We saw each other. We came close and shook each other's hand. He said, "You look hot." Replied, "I need a shower."

We took the L back Williamsburg. Hu Chin lived two blocks from Bedford. There were hipsters everywhere. Hu Chin lived in a different apartment than before. It was a nice size and clean. John Walters and his girlfriend lived in it. I had never met his girlfriend. The news was, she was Korean, small, and had a positive attitude. John Walters and his girlfriend who was named Katie were on a camping trip in Vermont.

Hu Chin showed me his computer. It was MAC laptop. Half the screen was gone. It was all fuzz. I said, "Hu, your screen is broke." He said, "I know, but I can still Gmail chat."

Took a shower. It was one of the best showers of my life. I used Hu Chin's organic body wash and tooth paste. Felt very clean.

Put fresh clothes on. Hu Chin showed me his bedroom. It was messy. There were 2500 copies of Jason Basini's new book. Hu Chin had published it. The boxes full of Jason's book were stacked higher than me. We looked at the boxes. Hu Chin said it would take ten years to sell 2500 poetry books. Told he had nothing else to do. He admitted that was true.

We sat at the kitchen table checking our emails. Then we left. It was night. The streets of Williamsburg were full of hipsters. We went to go see Andrew and his roommate Tod. Tod was a doctor of computer science who changed life goals and wanted to be a writer.

Ended up on Bedford at Mexican Place. Full of hipsters. Everyone seemed happy, it was summer, people were drinking. Andrew was now working for a major publishing company in a small office. He complained about it. It did sound lame. But it was obvious that he would move up in the future and his current lameness would end. Tod was interning at The New Yorker and getting an MFA from NYU. Andrew had his MFA from Columbia.

Andrew talked about restaurants. Hu Chin and Andrew fought over the remnants of the nachos. I drank water, they drank beer.

We went to a bar down the street. More hipsters. A lot of people. Friday night on Bedford. We walked to the back of the bar. It was an open patio. People were smoking and drinking. Andrew was talking to a group of people. He didn't introduce Hu Chin and I. Tod talked to us. Hu Chin and I sat on a small wooden thing. We were very close. There were no else to sit. We didn't get beers. An attractive Asian man came in, with a perfectly shaved face and nicely combed hair. Hu and I looked at him, Hu said, "That guy is the best person in this bar." I said, "Look how he listens, look how he laughs right at the perfect time." Hu chin said, "He is really good at being a person." Then we named the guy Kevin. Then we pretended we were Kevin and talked to each other listening intently, looking at each other's eyes, responding with witty yet informative things. It was funny. Andrew came over to us and told us we needed to sit in certain spots so everyone could sit facing each other. We sat down. There was a girl who worked on Broadway next to me. Everything she said was really loud. All Hu Chin and I wanted to do was pretend we were Keven.

We all left. On the sidewalk Hu Chin and I pretended we were Kevin more. We went to Andrew and Tod' apartment. Andrew gave me a copy of his magazine he created. It was a really nice magazine. It was large and the printing looked good. Some of the poetry in it was even good. Tod showed us an article he wrote concerning computers, it had graphs.

There were women there but Hu and I didn't talk to them. Hu had gotten a girlfriend who went to NYU. She was at home in Pittsburgh. I just didn't care.

Hu Chin and I went back to his apartment. We sat at his kitchen table. Talked about Jason Bassini. Jason Bassini had just made a video for Youtube. He looked gray and sickly. He could barely talk. Bassini looked like he might die. We imagine Bassini in first person:

I am going to the bathroom.

I am walking down the hall of a small Seattle apartment.

I need pay my rent. My rent must be paid.

Crushed underneath the rent.

I am going to brush my teeth.

I am looking at my toothbrush on the counter.

I am holding my toothbrush.

I put toothpaste on the toothbrush.

I am lifting the toothbrush to my mouth.

I am now cleaning my teeth.

I am Jason Bassini.

I work as a person that sells clothes on the sidewalks of Seattle.

Hu Chin and I talk about Jason Bassini pushing his grocery cart full of clothes down the streets of Seattle, probably all sweating and pissed off. One of the wheels of the cart hits a crack, it falls over, the clothes spill. Jason Bassini all sweaty, cursing his Catholic God, picking up the clothes that fell out and putting them back in the cart. Jason sitting beside his clothes reading a Lydia Davis novel, most of the time just staring into space. He wipes sweat off his forehead.

Next morning, woke up, early. Sat and read *Trout Fishing in America*. Noticed they had a patio. Went on patio. Sat on patio. Noticed there were plants. Looked at the plants.   There were a lot of herbs, no tomatoes or peppers. Giant nautical star hanging. Went back inside. Went back to sleep. Woke again to Hu Chin walking around.

Hu Chin and I go to Manahattan on L. I leave Hu Chin. Hu Chin goes to NYU library. I get on Q, head to Coney Island. Sit on Q and read *Adderall Diaries* by Elliot. The book is okay, everything is okay. Subway emerges from underneath the earth. Stop reading and look around at Brooklyn. The neighborhoods look like they were built 100 years ago. A group of black people get on the subway, three sets of couples. They all seem happy. Everyone is happy. Get to Coney Island. Walk down the street. There are thousands of people, mostly Latinos. Walk to beach first. There was the ocean. It was large and blue. The wind hit me hard. Loved the wind. There was no wind in the city. Feeling the wind was good. Large boardwalk selling lots of food and beer. Didn't go to Nathan's, the line was too long. Went to another place with no line, ordered a steak sandwich with sweet not hot peppers and no onions. They put onions on it anyway. Walked up boardwalk, sat on bench next a Latino man. He was speaking Spanish to somebody on his cell phone. His six year old son kept yelling at him, "Can I take my shoes off." His father wasn't listening. His father kept talking on his cell phone. The child said again, "Daddy, let me take off my shoes. I want to run in the sand with no shoes." His father kept talking on cell phone. The kid yelled, "Daddy, let me take off my shoes!" The dad said without looking up at the boy, "Yeah, whatever." The boy took his shoes and socks. The boy was very happy.

Two gay men in very short shorts were playing volleyball together. They weren't exactly playing. They seemed to be practicing serving just in case a game got started.

Walked down the boardwalk, saw dancing. There were people dancing to very bad techno music. There was a cute Asian dancing wearing a Coney Island dance shirt. I wanted to touch her ass.

Walked back down to the bathrooms. Park rangers were standing together. Arab men were sitting down together sweating looking bored. Old Latinos sat on lawn chairs trying to sell goods. I took a shit in the bathroom. Walked to the fenced-in area where the merchants were. They were selling cheap shit. I didn't have enough money to buy any of it. Bought an empanada. It was a meat empanada not a cheese empanada.

Got back on subway. Arrived in Manahattan. Sat in Think Coffee for an hour. Drank an iced coffee. Everyone had a MAC. There were MACs everywhere. Glowing apples abound. Started to fear the MACs would come alive and attack in unison. There was a girl who did not have a MAC. She hated herself. Tegan and Sara and Beirut played on the radio.

Went to Washington Square Park. Wrote text message to Hu. Hu Chin comes out. We go to dinner at Klong. Lin was going to be there. Lin and I had made up.   We wrote emails. The emails said nice things. We became friends again. She was dating a French man.

A man named Louis Russo was coming. He met Hu and I outside of the NYU library. He worked for a local television station. He seemed nervous and sad. Hu Chin was building an army of sad depressed grown men. This army of sad depressed grown men would one day conquer the world and force everyone to read Richard Yates and Jean Rhys. There would be no war because everyone would be too depressed to care about marching and doing push ups. There would be famine though because everyone would be too depressed to garden and work very hard at anything.

We met Lin at Saint Marks. She was with two French men. Her boyfriend was a happy French man named Etienne. Etienne was taller, with a nice collar shirt, and very spunky for a man. The other French man was short, and sad looking. No one told me his name.

Lin's hair was long. She looked older, her face wasn't so innocent. Cat Steven's *Wild World* played in my head.

Went to Klong. It was nice inside. It was busy. I didn't know what anything was on the menu. Hu Chin told me, I listened and ordered. Lin talked about Bernie Madoff. No one could remember exactly how much he stole, one person said 48 billion, another 57 billion, another 51 billion, the actual number is 65 billion. No one could figure out how one could steal billions of dollars and where would you hide it.

Etienne kept pretending to be surprised. It was really funny. Lin kept acting embarrassed which made it even funnier. Hu, Louis and I kept laughing hysterically. The other nameless French man sat quietly text messaging. Lin kept saying, "Please forgive him, he's French. I think they are all fucked up. I don't understand a damn thing he is doing or saying half the time."

Everyone kept laughing. Etienne kept pretending he was seeing something shocking. He kept waving his arms about and making his eyes huge. Lin kept acting more and more embarrassed and talking about how French people had no sense of humor and something was wrong with them.

We ate dinner, went outside and stood on Saint Mark's. Tom White's apartment was across the street but he was sick. Lin and her French men went somewhere. Louis, Hu, and I went back to Williamsburg. When we got back to apartment John Walters and his girlfriend Katie were there. Katie was Korean-American, small and adorable. She had a positive attitude. Happy to see somebody okay and stable living with Hu and John, they both needed a positive influence.

John Walters wasn't drunk. He was weird but not as loud and conquering. He poured me a cup of scotch. He put seltzer water and ice cubes in it. Louis drank from a bottle of wine. Katie showed me her plants outside. Katie and I sat outside on chairs and talked about plants. Gave plant growing advice. She smiled a lot. It was nice to see someone smiling. Went back in. John Walters and Katie went to his bedroom and watched a movie on his computer. Louis, Hu, and I sat at the kitchen table. Louis asked Hu, "What kind of music did your parents listen to?" Hu responded, "Traditional Chinese music." Louis and I talked about sports and our parents. Hu Gmail chatted with his girlfriend. Louis and I went outside and smoked a cigarette. Louis gave me two dollars for one my cigarettes. I took the two dollars.

Went to sleep.

Woke up Katie moving around in the kitchen. Katie said she needed to go to work. She worked at an art gallery doing something. Don't know what she did. John Walters got up soon after that. We went downstairs, walked down the street and got coffee. Went back to apartment, sat on patio and played cards. Told him I got a blowjob from Petra. He said that was cool. Talked about things we needed to do in life. He beat me at Rummy. We walked to a park. There were Latinos playing baseball. We sat on a bench. He told me he loved Katie, it seemed like he did. He said he wanted to be a famous writer. I told him I liked his new poetry book. He told me he rejected Hu Chin. We thought it was funny. Walked back to the apartment. John said he had to piss. When we got back he left. He had to walk dogs.

Hu Chin woke up shortly after. We took the L to Manhattan. Went to small grocery store. A tall black man with dreads made Hu Chin a coconut shake. Sat in Washington Square Park on a bench in the shade. Two pretty Russian girls played on a skate board in front of us. A band played, made up of four white guys. An overweight white man holding a cell phone stood by dancing. A black man looking old and angry drove a lawn mower throw the park. Thousands of people were walking around. Old women from Park Slope were sitting by us waiting to die. One of them had their very own middle-aged black woman as a personal nurse. Hu and I did nothing but sit there and talked about writing and how to become famous writers. We sat for several hours talking. We went to Think Coffee several times to get iced coffees. Hu eventually went to NYU library. Walked around and sat in the park for two hours. Felt disoriented and terrible. Too much stimuli, too much walking, no anchor in reality. Needed to get back on the bus, back to Ohio, where reality made sense. Stumbled into American Apparel trying to make sense of my life, but no sense came. Sat in Shakespeare and Company reading Rorty, still no sense came. Hu Chin came up out of NYU. We ate Asian food. He had soup, I had Lo Mein and chicken. He could tell I was tired. We talked softly about polite things. We took the subway to Port Authority. Walked around in it, trying to find where I needed to be. We went to a Duane Reade to get water and chips.

Back on the bus. Going home to Ohio. Surrounded by poor Latinos, blacks, and Asians. Got a text message on my cell phone from Tony, it said, "Unstable, broke up with girlfriend just now." "Who that girl Ashley?" "Yeah, Ashley." I laughed. Couldn't sleep on the bus. Everything was dramatic and weird. The sun came up, lighting up the bus. Everyone was sleeping. Looked out the window.

illustration by Phillip Huddleston

About the author:

Noah Cicero is the author of *The Human War* (Fugue State Press, 2003), *The Condemned* (Six Gallery Press, 2006), *Burning Babies* (Parlor Press, 2006), *Treatise* (A-Head Publishing, 2008), and *The Insurgent* (Blatt, 2010). Since its release, The Human War has become a favorite of the literary underground and is being adapted to film. This is his sixth novel.